The Monsters Within

Corvus Winchester

ISBN-10: 0615830226
ISBN-13: 978-0615830223 (MidKnight Publishing)

DEDICATION

First of all I dedicate this book to my Lord. Without Him I would not be here and this book would be completely impossible. I thank him for our salvation every day and am so glad to be his child. Second, I would like to thank my family for being so supportive of my writing ventures and here's to hoping for many more titles.

CONTENTS

'He has redeemed my soul from going to the pit, And my life shall see the light.'

Job 33:28

Corvus Winchester

1

"This is it?" Ethan grumbled as he stared out of the fingerprint streaked car window.

"It looks so." His father, Travis, said in a husky sigh.

Ethan pulled his ear buds from his ears and began to roll them around his fingers. He looked up at his mother sitting in the passenger seat of their rundown Oldsmobile. Her head rested heavily on her fingers as she stared away from the house.

"They still aren't talking. No surprise there." Travis thought silently, as he unbuckled his seatbelt.

"Well are we going to do this, or what?" Travis asked her firmly.

She continued to stare out the passenger side window, ignoring his question. She bit down on her bottom lip as her eyes narrowed. Her delicate hand anxiously rubbed her bare ring finger, as she had removed the piece days earlier.

"I'm tired of this attitude Katherine. I'm trying." Travis forced a hard lump down his throat, before continuing. "We couldn't stay in that house. We . . . We just couldn't."

She turned to face him in a fit of anger. Tears streamed down her red cheeks as she stared at him in a burning rage. "I could've stayed! I could've. You need this! Not me!"

"I'm trying! Okay? I'm trying to make things better!" Travis growled.

Ethan rolled his eyes, as he watched the two argue. He rubbed his sore forearms and pulled his long sleeves even farther down his arms. He pulled at the sleeves, stretching the fabric farther and farther with every scream.

"Oh, yeah? Well, why don't you go run back to your little hussy?" Katherine remarked in a fit of rage.

"I told you nothing happened. Nothing!" Travis grabbed her shoulder. "But you still won't belie . . ."

He was stopped by a knocking sound peppering the driver's side window in an energetic fashion. The occupants of the car turned to see a smiling, red headed sales agent in her mid-forties, waving to the family.

The three collected themselves quickly and began to exit the car slowly. Katherine wiped her tears away with the sleeves of her cream cardigan. Her dark brown hair blew across her face violently in the summer breeze.

Ethan shook his head as his parents shot menacing glares at each other from across the car. They hadn't talked in over sixteen hours. He had forced himself to tolerate every silent moment during the car ride. Never once did they acknowledge him in the backseat. Not even once.

"Hi, I'm Evelyn Wiles." The real estate agent extended her hand towards Travis. "I assume your Mr. Holloway."

"I am." He faked a smile and shook the woman's soft hand.

"Well, why don't I show you around?" She grinned wryly, before starting up the cobblestone entryway.

Ms. Wiles pulled a key from her jacket pocket and began to unlock the gate. The unique wrought-iron gate was the only entrance inside the stone wall that wrapped around the entire property line. On the right side of the gate was a plaque fixed to the mighty stone wall. The plaque was written in Spanish with fading engraved letters, reading: Casa de la redención. The gate swung open to a cobblestone path matching the front steps and led straight to the mahogany front door.

The door was only one distinctive piece exclusive to this unique Victorian style house. The two and a half story residence towered over the surrounding houses of the neighborhood. It had obviously been here long before there was any other construction in the vicinity.

The inside of the house was breathtaking as solid wood panels lined the walls. From the foyer, the Holloways noticed the house included a study, a library, and a large walk-in pantry. They walked around the large house speechlessly. A fact that did not surprise Ethan, but this was a different kind of silence. This was an amazed silence. Something they could both agree on.

Ethan snuck off from the group and decided to tour the house alone. He snuck through the library and scurried about the main floor, like a rat learning its new surroundings. He opened almost every door and cabinet, curious to know what was inside. The basement door gave him the most trouble.

On the first try, it seemed to be locked. But with more and more effort, the lock gave way. He slowly turned the antique knob and peered down into the dark cellar. Smells of must and decay rose up from the dank basement. He toyed with the idea of taking a few steps down the old staircase, but wondered if they would splinter under his weight.

He began to turn back, when he caught a blur of movement out of the corner of his eye. He slowly turned back and crouched low onto the first step. The wood step squeaked with pressure as he shifted more of his weight onto it. He peered into the cellar, but all was dark in the smelly basement.

His hand slid up the wall, searching for a light switch. There was nothing. He couldn't find a switch on either side of the wall. He began to think what he had seen was just his imagination playing tricks with him, when the sound of a tin can falling on the concrete floor of the basement resonated up the staircase. He gasped and paused for a moment. He was frozen in terror.

Ethan's eyes narrowed as he swallowed a large lump in his throat. He lifted his left foot and felt behind him for the main floor. His foot made contact with the hardwood floor and he slowly stepped back into the foyer. His hands brushed along the sides of the doorframe, cautiously stabilizing him.

The fingers of his right hand brushed along the strike plate of the door jam. Its unusual texture caught his attention as his eyes continued to remain affixed at the bottom of the staircase. He pulled his eyes away, quick enough to notice; the plate appeared to have been melted.

The metal was solidified in a state reminding Ethan of dripping wax solidified on a candle. Drops of metal lined the plate, embossed into the door frame. Perhaps this is why the door was so hard to open, Ethan thought to himself, quickly closing the cellar door.

In the study, Ms. Wiles continued to show Travis and

Katherine the library. Old classics lined the walls and appeared untouched for years. A fine amount of dust was still noticeable between the edges of the hard covers. Travis smirked as it was clear the real estate agency had missed cleaning such a detailed space.

"As you can see, most of the previous owners' belongings still remain in the house." Ms. Wiles waved her hand across the room, motioning towards the aging books.

"If I may ask, what happened to the previous owners?" Katherine asked inquisitively.

"They disappeared from the house. Bills began to pile up in the mailbox," Ms. Wiles explained, pursing her thin lips. "They weren't seen from neighbors or family and pretty soon the house returned to the bank."

"That wouldn't have any reason to do with the price of the house, would it?" Travis smiled jokingly.

"I'm afraid it might." Ms. Wiles smiled, leaning against the solid cherry desk. "You see, most people think they were having problems and ran away from here."

"It's too bad. They were such kind folks as well." Ms. Wiles head fell in remembrance of them.

"That's an unusual painting." Katherine remarked as she noticed an antique painting hanging in between two of the bookshelves.

The painting was of a tree standing tall in the middle of paradise. Luscious red fruit hung from its branches, blowing in the breeze. A naked woman was depicted being pushed away from the tree by an equally naked man. The character's faces were shown in agony as the man pulled her farther away from the tree. Both of the woman's arms reached for the tree, longing to touch it.

In her right hand was a fruit of the same shape as that on the tree, except for this fruit was rotten. It was black and decaying in her hand as her fingers tightly clutched it. Pieces of the fruit began to fall from her hand poisoning the ground below them, turning the grass black and grey.

"Yes. The previous man of the house admired this piece for some reason." Ms. Wiles stared at the painting, as a curious amount of sadness began to appear in her eyes. "I tried to convince him that the piece did not fit with the artistic style of the house, but he insisted."

Ethan could hear the voices of his parents from the foyer as he crept up the wooden staircase. He quickly shuffled up the stairs, being careful to not make them creak. Once he reached the top floor, he explored each room inside and out.

For the most part, they were all identical. Some were larger than others and most included furniture still, but together they were a collection of lifeless rooms. There were easily three bedrooms on the top floor. This did not include the nursery, for which Ethan was too nervous to enter.

The nursery still included a baby's crib, handmade and polished. He expected to hear a cry from the crib or something similar, like those he had seen in horror films. He opened the closet in the hallway and inspected the shelves. White linens and sheets lie neatly arranged on each of the shelves. He closed the door in boredom.

Beside the closet was the door to a dumbwaiter. He smiled slightly as he opened the door. To his disappointment the lift was at a lower floor. Ethan peered down into the dark shaft curiously. Nothing could be made out in the dark shaft descending into nothingness. Ethan pulled at the rope, but it remained stuck. In disappointment, Ethan quickly gave up and shut the door.

The afternoon sun cast shadows on the wall as Ethan's silhouette towered over those of the rails and staircase. He flicked the switch on the wall to turn on the hallway lights, but nothing happened. He realized that the real estate agency probably wasn't paying the electricity bill or perhaps a breaker was blown. That would just mean his father would have to go into the dark basement. Ethan smiled at the idea.

Ethan began to debate returning to the group, when something stopped him. It wasn't as if he had stopped walking for a moment. No, this was like something was holding him in place. It was almost as if he was frozen in place without the use of his legs. He looked down at his feet and nothing but shadows covered them. The dark hallway was empty. Nothing was holding him there.

He watched as Ms. Wiles led his parents across the foyer through a pair of swinging double-wide doors. Ethan stood silent as he watched them pass, being careful to not alert them to his sneaking about. Although, he was sure they knew he was gone already - they probably didn't care. Perhaps they didn't even remember they had brought him along. For all they cared, they could have left him in Los Angeles.

"And here is the kitchen!" Ms. Wiles announced proudly as she brushed her hand along the marble countertop.

The kitchen included a new refrigerator and beautiful

cherry cabinets. Katherine inspected the leather barstools set around the island centered directly in the middle of the kitchen. Travis opened the tall, metallic refrigerator doors.

"Man, we could fit lots of sausages in here honey!" Travis leaned back, smiling at Katherine.

Katherine quickly shot him an angered glance across the island.

"Katherine loves sausages." Travis chuckled to Ms. Wiles as he closed the refrigerator doors.

"Not as much as Travis loves his donuts." Katherine faked a smile, back in his direction. "Right, honey? All soft and warm. I'm sure you'd love to stick your . . ."

Travis sighed, interrupting Katherine's rant as he leaned onto the marble island. "Sausages used to be one of Katherine's comfort foods, before she . . ."

"Before I put myself into a phat camp." She snarled, shaking her head at the bad memories. "I used to surround myself with comfort foods."

"You should've seen our grocery bill." Travis smirked again.

"I wonder why I needed comfort!" Katherine retorted sarcastically as she passed behind Ms. Wiles. "Maybe I never felt secure, unlike your little freshmen skanks!"

"Well!" Ms. Wiles interjected with a smile, intentionally disturbing the rising tension. "I think you look lovely, Mrs. Holloway."

"Thank you, Ms. Wiles." Katherine smiled as she brushed her paisley dress back over her finely trimmed waist.

Atop the staircase, Ethan continued to try commanding his legs to lift, to swing, to do anything. Something continued to hold him in place. His legs remained frozen in place as he squirmed about. He could move freely from his waist up, but it was as if something had tightly wrapped itself around his legs and fixed them to the landing!

2

Ethan peered over the balcony, to the empty foyer. His voice tried to call out as loud as he could, but his mouth felt as if it was sealed shut. Not a sound escaped him. Not even a peep. He tried to stretch open his jaw, but his entire face felt tired and weak.

Inaudible whispers began to fill his ears. He turned his head to see where the noise was coming from. The hallway was completely empty. Nothing was even close to him, but the whispers began to escalate. Suddenly, there were several sounds. Like multiple people whispering right into his ears, in a foreign language of some kind.

The whispers fought over one another, each trying to be louder than the last. Their voices hissed and scrambled in his ears as they continued to whisper over each other. Some sounded as if they were arguing with another voice as others tried to talk directly to Ethan. Ethan felt as if his head was going to explode. The voices became louder and louder with increasing intensity, before suddenly falling silent.

Ethan looked around. It was as if he had become deaf. Not a bird's chirp or a board's creek could be heard throughout the entire house. Everything was silent. He noticed a mirror on the wall. He turned to face the mirror and cried at the sight he saw in it. His mouth was melting into one piece. His lips began to disappear as the flesh around them began to form over where his lips used to be.

He leaned towards the mirror, feet frozen in place. He caught a movement in the reflection, behind him. He spun around at the waist, but the hallway was still empty. He turned back towards the mirror. His pupils were becoming darker. Their hazel color was quickly being consumed by a dark cloudy substance.

He squirmed at the waist commanding his feet to step down the stairs. His feet remained frozen in place. His arms felt like dead weights at his sides. He tried to scream as loud as possible, but only a slightly muffled squeak came from his voice. He turned back towards the mirror and his heart stopped for a moment as a long-haired man with a sinister smile stood behind him.

Ethan spun around. His feet unexpectedly flew out from under him, as they were no longer held captive. He tumbled head first down the staircase. His arms flailed about searching for anything to grab. His back slammed into the wall, before landing roughly on the hard mahogany floor of the foyer.

His parents rushed into the room with Ms. Wiles close behind them. His cheeks flushed in embarrassment as he groaned in pain. He looked up toward the top of the staircase for the man he had seen behind him, but the hallway remained empty.

"What happened?" Travis demanded as he picked Ethan up off the floor.

"I . . . I" Ethan's fingers reached for his mouth, feeling his separate lips now able to speak.

"We're sorry. He's been a little on edge with the move." Katherine apologized to Ms. Wiles.

"It's quite all right. The young ones are always the most naïve." She smiled as she shifted a stack of papers underneath her left arm.

"Well, I'll get these filed. Welcome home, Mr. and Mrs. Holloway." Ms. Wiles smiled as she handed Katherine the key to the house. "Welcome home, Ethan."

Her steely grey eyes glowered at him with a sneering smile. "Good day." She waved, as she shuffled over to the front door. She paused for a moment at the front door and turned to lock eyes with Travis. Her thin lips grew into a wide smile and nodded gently before stepping outside. She took one more look at the family before closing the heavy wooden door behind her.

"Really?" Katherine huffed, staring at Travis.

"What?" Travis' eyes widened as Katherine glared at him.

"Her? You're flirting with *that*?" She motioned towards the no longer present Ms. Wiles.

"Ew! I was not flirting with her!" Travis stammered with disbelief.

"I saw you throughout the tour." Katherine cried as she stomped into the kitchen. "You're unbelievable!"

"You signed those papers? You bought the house and you didn't even ask me?" Ethan growled with disgust, tears forming in his eyes. "There's something wrong with this house! Something really wrong!"

"Not now, Ethan." Travis brushed his hands angrily through his neatly combed hair.

"Of course! Not ever." Ethan forced back tears as he shook his head in disgust. "You never care what I think!"

Ethan stormed across the foyer and swung the front door open. He growled in disgust, before powerfully slamming the door behind himself.

"Ethan!" Travis called after him. He sighed in exhaustion.

The move wasn't supposed to be this hard. After everything

that happened last summer, the entire family needed a fresh start. Of course, Adriana *had* to flirt with him this semester. Especially at *that* time. There are always one or two freshmen that think they can get an easy A from their teacher.

Travis wasn't like that though. These kids are just babies to him. They try to be flirtatious and sexy. They try coming on to teachers to make their lives just a little bit easier by selling a part of themselves. It made Travis's stomach sink to even think about what those young girls are doing to their lives.

Travis smiled as he noticed the antiquated fireplace. Cold chills had been shooting up and down his spine, ever since he got out of the car. He couldn't tell if it was excitement or nervous energy from being somewhere completely different. Maybe it was knowing that Katherine would probably make him spend the entire night on the couch. No, this was something else. Something very different.

Night fell silently upon the house. Ethan had not returned and Travis continued to sit in the lounge, staring intensely at the kindling fire. Katherine was hard at work in the master bedroom unpacking the few boxes they had brought in the car with them.

They only contained a few of the necessities. A hairdryer, soap, some food, an aging coffee pot, and other miscellaneous items. She quietly moaned as she bit into a power bar. It was the first thing she had eaten all day, after that terrible egg and cheese biscuit from the drive-thru this morning. She enjoyed the moment as her mouth came alive with the taste of peanut butter and chocolate.

She lied back on the master bed and closed her eyes. She couldn't believe Travis' nerve. After all they had been through she couldn't believe his ignorance. In spite of his determination to make everything right, she couldn't find it in herself to forgive him. Not for those things. Not for *that* incident.

Tears began to swell in her eyes before she quickly blinked them away. She lie silent, staring at the dull grey ceiling. She hadn't wanted to move. *He* was in their old house, not this one. Travis thought the entire family needed space from what had happened, so he quit his old job and moved them halfway across the country.

This wasn't what she needed. She needed to still feel his presence. To still be there in that kitchen waiting for him to come down the stairs in the morning. She stifled a sniffle as she wiped a tear from her cheek. That house was his. But now they abandoned him. She was afraid she'd forget the way he used to laugh. She didn't want to forget that. She didn't want to forget him.

Katherine sat up and brushed her long brown hair behind her neck. She turned on the light for the bathroom and sighed. Nothing happened. She flipped the switch again and still the lights remained unlit. She tried once more and the bulbs flickered to life.

Katherine walked over to the sink and washed her face. This house was old. She didn't like the unreliability of it. She felt scared being alone in such a large house. She never felt that way in their old house. This house just felt eerie in some way. Maybe it was the shadows in the halls, or maybe it was just the house.

She stood back up and looked at her tired face in the mirror. She rubbed the dark circles under her eyes hoping they would disappear. Katherine frowned at her reflection and stared deep into her green eyes.

"I don't forgive you either." She murmured at the reflection.

She bent over the sink again, splashing the cold water over her tired eyes. She stood back up and half expected something to appear behind her. This house was creepy enough.

She switched off the faucet and turned to fill the bathtub. She walked back into the master bedroom and pulled off her cardigan, before tossing it on the bed. She wiggled out of her paisley dress and left it lying on the hardwood floor as she gingerly walked back into the bathroom.

Outside the house, Ethan sighed in depression as he set his head against the cold metal wall of the gardening shed. He felt like he needed to keep his distance from the family. That way they could sort out all of their issues on their own. It really didn't matter if he was there or not. But at least out here, most of their yelling could not be heard among the various tools and lawn care equipment.

He closed his eyes as he pulled a small black case from his back pocket. His fingers brushed against the side of the credit card-sized case, feeling for the familiar latch. He opened his eyes as the case snapped open.

Ethan's brow furled as his fingers lightly grabbed the thin object inside the case. It was a small, thin steel razor blade. It was slightly stained from prior use, but remained sterile and clean. He sniffled as thoughts of anger raced through his mind.

He needed to feel. He didn't feel loved or needed by anyone or anything. Kids at school always laughed about the incident and called him names. That was one thing Ethan didn't miss about home. One of several things he didn't miss about his old home.

In some ways he was glad they had moved. But he began to question his sanity after what had happened at the top of the stairs. Maybe the move was affecting him in some ways too. Perhaps being frozen in place was just his way of telling himself he's stuck between his feuding parents. It was probably the stress. Maybe it was being so far away from their old house. Would *he* have approved of the family leaving him?

Ethan shook his head. He tried not to think about what had happened. He replaced those thoughts with the terrifying image of the man he had seen in the mirror. Something must have been wrong with him. Ethan hadn't felt scared or terrified when those things were happening. He was just trapped. Uncontrollably trapped.

A tear slid down Ethan's cheek as he stared at the razor blade. He didn't feel. What was going on with him? His cares, his worries, his life was deadened. It had no feeling. He felt hollow inside. Like he was empty. Like all of what he used to be was fading or being sucked into a black hole inside of himself.

His senses never felt alive. He didn't feel joy or happiness. He barely felt anything at all, except anger. He could feel anger. He could feel anger towards his parents, towards the kids at school. He felt angry at the entire world. But for what reason?

Ethan felt another tear slide down his cheek as he stared at the blade. What did this life offer? What is life without feeling? When the world is grey and without hope, what reason is there to live? He looked through the small dirty window towards the house. The only light he could see was the small flicker of the fireplace in the living room.

Where was the light to drag him out of this? Ethan shook his head and swallowed a hard lump in his throat. He was tired of not feeling anything. He felt distant from the world. Everyone else was always caught up in their daily chores. They cared what other people thought. They cared about the people around them. They cared about the events in their lives. Ethan just wanted to care.

He pulled the sleeves of his shirt up to his elbows. He took one more look at the blade and sighed. His forearms were covered in scars. They were sore. He could still pick out the newest set from when he had made the excuse to use the restroom while his parents were ordering drive-thru this morning.

Ethan sneered in disgust at the very thought of his parents. He held back the tears swelling in his eyes and wiped away those running down his cheeks. This was the only way he felt anything. He could feel pain. Not just the emotional pain he always felt, but actual physical pain. It brought him outside of those feelings. It allowed him to feel. Ethan took one more deep breath and paused for a moment. He let the breath out and then slid the razor blade across his forearm.

Inside the house, Katherine had just found the right temperature for her bath. It had taken minutes for the water to warm to the right temperature. She didn't want to freeze, but she also didn't want to have the water scald her.

She smiled slightly as she slowly dipped her toe in the water. It was finally just right. Katherine slowly slid into the bath holding both sides of the ceramic tub. She sighed in pleasure as the warm water surrounded her body. Her cold skin began to regain warmth as she lay in the tub.

It had been a long time since she was able to get in the water. After the incident, something about water scared her. She had always been scared of swimming in large bodies of water, but this was different. This wasn't about drowning. This was terrifying at first. It reminded her of him. Katherine realized she needed to face her fears.

She couldn't be afraid her entire life. She blamed herself partly for what had happened. She couldn't come to forgive herself. She was right there! She could've stopped the entire thing! If only she had realized what was happening. If only she wasn't afraid of the water.

She was dying inside. She could still feel the stinging pain as she saw the events unfold before her very eyes. She told herself there was nothing she could've done, but she knew that was a lie. The blame still lies on her. She blamed Travis as well. He could've done something. This ordeal had been in his hands.

Katherine gasped as something suddenly wrapped around her throat, choking her with incredible strength. Katherine quickly looked around the bathroom. There was nothing in the bathroom. She choked as she tried to feel if someone was behind her. There was nothing. It was just the air.

The object wrapped around her throat and began to pull tighter as she struggled against the unseen force. Katherine's head dipped below the water. She quickly grabbed the sides of the tub and pulled herself up out of the water. She gasped for air as the object around her throat released its grip.

Her eyes nervously darted around the room. There was nothing in the room. There was nothing in the tub besides water. What was going on? Her breath shook as she tried to regain her air. What was going on? What was that?

In an instant, her whole body was grabbed by an unseen force beneath the water and pulled under. She quickly grabbed a breath of air before being completely submerged in the bath. She flailed her arms wildly around her body, hoping to make contact with the object as she held her breath.

She slid her hands down her hips and around her back. There was nothing tangible. She couldn't make contact with anything. The only thing around her was water, but something was pulling her down. She opened her eyes to see a bright light above the water.

The force released her and she floated in the aquatic abyss. Her surroundings were much larger than that of the tub. It seemed familiar to her. She was immersed in something far bigger. Something without boundaries. What was happening? Where was she?

Out of the corner of her eye, she spotted an object. She turned to examine it. It was a small boy floating in the water. His blonde hair suspended in the water as he kept himself afloat. She cried as she recognized the boy. She covered her mouth quickly before too much air escaped.

The boy smiled at her. She felt so happy she wanted to cry. It was him! He was alive! Katherine began to try to swim over to the boy, but something grabbed her foot. She tried to swim harder as the object wrapped even tighter around her ankle. It began to pull her deeper. She gasped as the remaining air in her body escaped her lungs.

She was being pulled deeper and deeper. The light began to fade as she was quickly consumed in total darkness. She struggled and tried to grab her ankle, but she was being pulled too quickly. "No! No!" she thought as she was pulled away from the boy.

She saw him! He was right there. She could save him! She could do something this time! She struggled against the force. Pulling, pushing herself; she tried everything possible. In the blink of an eye, she sat up, gasping for air.

Her hands desperately clutched the sides of the tub as her whole body began to shake. "No! No! No! No!" she yelled aloud. She was back in the bathroom. She stood up and looked at the tub underneath her. She knelt down, searching the bottom of the tub, feeling for anything. Her hands fluttered about as she felt the floor and walls of the tub.

"No! Please!" Katherine sobbed into her hands.

The water began circling the drain as she dropped to her knees in the ceramic tub. She began to rock herself for comfort as her lips trembled. Her forehead pressed against the bottom of the tub with every rocking motion she made. She continued to sob as the cold air nipped at her wet body.

"Are you okay?" Travis cried as he rushed into the bathroom.

He slid slightly across the wet bathroom floor, falling to his knees beside the tub. He wrapped his muscular arm around her shaking body in comfort. He swallowed deeply as he stared at her tear streaked face.

"What happened?" Travis asked with genuine concern. "Tell me."

Katherine sniffled and wiped her face with her wet hand. "I saw him. He was alive."

"You know he's not." Travis held back tears of his own as he forced back painful memories from flooding into his mind.

"Yes, he was. I saw him." She uttered before erupting into

more tears.

Travis helped sit his wife up and grabbed a towel from the shelf. He climbed into the tub behind her and wrapped the towel around her shoulders. She trembled as she softly lied back onto his firm chest. Travis wrapped his arms around her and kissed her forehead.

"Shh. Shh. Shh." He uttered as he brushed her wet hair away from her face. "I miss him too, sweetheart. I miss him too."

"Christian," she cried as she clutched tightly to the front of Travis' shirt.

Travis forced back tears as he watched his wife tremble in his arms. He brushed her hair back and kissed the top of her head.

"It's okay. We'll get through this." Travis whispered. "Everything will be alright."

Corvus Winchester

3

.

Ethan breathed in a deep sigh as he slid the black case into his back pocket again. He pulled the sleeves of his shirt down around his arms and winced as the sleeves brushed along the fresh scars. He slowly opened the door of the shed and stopped as it began to creak.

He pushed the door open just a crack further and slipped through. He shut the noisy door behind him and flipped the latch. He jiggled the door slightly to make sure it was locked.

"Whatta ya doin'?" A perky, but curious voice called from behind him.

Ethan quickly whirled around and stumbled back into the shed doors. His eyes caught sight of a beautiful red-head twenty-year old girl. A smile quickly spread across her face as her green eyes glistened in the moonlight.

"What? Where?" Ethan stammered as he tried to calm himself. "Where did you come from? Who are you?"

"The name's Emily." The girl stuck her hand out, smiling even more.

"Come on, I won't bite." She laughed as Ethan hesitantly reached out to shake her hand.

"And your name is . . ." her eyes widened in anticipation as she stared at Ethan inquisitively.

"Ethan . . . My name is Ethan." He smiled as he quickly regained himself.

"Nice to meet you Ethan," Emily smiled warmly as she pulled her green hoodie over her head.

"Where did you come from?" Ethan asked questioningly.

"Where do we all come from?" She giggled as she pointed upwards. "But, if you wanna know where I live. I'm your neighbor. Just don't get any fresh ideas."

Ethan raised his right eyebrow as Emily started to walk towards the back yard.

"Do you always come on to other people's property like this?" Ethan asked, uncontrollably entranced by this strange girl.

"Do you always ask so many questions?" She laughed as she knelt down to inspect the flower beds.

"Well, I don't usually find strange girls in my yard." He smirked as he watched her graceful fingers pluck a rose from the flower bed.

"You didn't find me, I found you." She pointed out as she

began to pull the petals from the rose.

"True." Ethan chuckled, before his expression turned into a frown. The thorns from the rose dug deep into her fingers as she continued to pluck the petals from the flower.

"You're bleeding!" Ethan stated, pointing to her hand.

"I know!" Emily's eyes flared with excitement and energy. "Don't you ever just want to feel alive?"

Ethan cautiously took a few steps back as he watched her turn back towards the flower beds. There was something strange about this girl that he found mesmerizing. He felt thrilled to meet someone his age, but there was a rare spark to this girl. She was unique in the most beautiful way.

"Have you discovered the paintings in the library yet?" Emily smiled as she hopped onto the small wall surrounding the garden.

"Paintings?" Ethan asked.

"Well, more like murals." She corrected as she walked along the wall. "The original owner's son or something drew them. Supposedly, he was disturbed and thought they were expressions of his pain or something."

"Interesting." Ethan smiled, raising a very curious eyebrow.

"How do you know about them?"

"Well, let's just say word gets around." She smiled, crouching enough to look him in the eyes. "Or maybe I lived here before."

"Did you?" Ethan asked as he watched her stand back up.

"Maybe. That's something you just have to guess about." Emily skipped along the garden wall and pulled herself up, onto the stone wall surrounding the property.

The large white moon illuminated her scarlet hair from behind her as she sat smiling at him atop the stone wall. She was amazing! She captivated him in a way that no one else had ever done before. He couldn't take his eyes off of her. She was so lively and full of vigor. He could tell that beneath the fiery persona she displayed, she was troubled much like him.

"Maybe I'm a ghost," She smiled. "Of some previous owner's daughter. Or maybe I'm one of the first owners of the house and now I've come to haunt you and pluck your roses."

"Maybe." Ethan smirked as he stared up at her.

"I've got to go now." She frowned as she glanced nervously over the wall. It was as if her parents were silently calling her home.

"But you just got here!" Ethan cried loudly.

"Shh!" Emily held up a finger to her lips. "It's like midnight or so."

"I won't tell if you don't." he gazed at her hopefully.

"I like you. You're cute." She smiled. "Maybe I'll come back. You seem like you're a nice guy."

"Oh, I am. I'm a super nice guy." Ethan stammered energetically.

"Ok, nice guy. See ya later!" She waved, before sliding herself off the wall into the adjacent yard.

"Wait!" Ethan hopped onto the garden wall and peered over the surrounding wall.

She was nowhere to be seen. She had disappeared somewhere into the cold night air. The neighboring yard was completely empty and without trace of the scarlet haired girl. Ethan smiled. He liked this new girl. There was something mysterious about her that intrigued him.

Ethan turned back and stepped down off of the garden wall. He noticed the rose she had plucked bare left lying on the garden wall. He picked it up carefully and smelled its remaining scent, hoping for further proof that she was real. He began to set it back on the garden wall, when he noticed something very disturbing.

The thorns protruding from the rose were covered with a black substance. It wasn't a dark red like blood. No, this was as black as oil. He frowned as he inspected the rest of the flower for where Emily had pricked her fingers. There wasn't a sign of blood. Only the beads of this strange black substance remained on the flower.

4

Travis awoke to a familiar sound. He groaned quietly as he shifted his body in the wooden antique rocker. He looked over to see Katherine sound asleep in the bed. He smiled as he pushed himself out of the hard chair.

He quietly stepped over to the side of the bed and pulled the white sheets up over her cold arms. He kissed her shoulder gently and pulled the covers the rest of the way up. Travis inhaled a deep breath as he watched his wife lie asleep in the bed.

He questioned why he had deserved this. If there was such a thing as a God, how could he allow his own wife to hate him for something he didn't even do? Perhaps, Travis was right when he married Katherine. Maybe she was too good for him. Maybe he didn't deserve a woman like her. She certainly didn't deserve a man like him.

Travis swallowed slowly as he watched her breathe. She was captivatingly beautiful. She always was. Even when her hair was a mess and she was fighting him, she was undeniably beautiful. He loved most everything about her, but she still had many traits that he disliked.

Among those many traits, was that of not letting go. She hadn't found it in her heart to forgive herself for what had happened. Travis could understand that she blamed him, but she also blamed herself. She was the closest to Christian.

His breath stopped for a moment as he heard the sound again. That sound was so familiar to him. The sound of a playful child. Not just any playful child. No, this was a special child. Travis crept to the bedroom door and slowly turned the knob.

The old mahogany door swung open quietly as he peered out into the hallway. There was nothing but darkness. He squinted down the staircase into the shadows. There was nothing.

The child laughed again, followed by a chorus of footsteps parading down the stairs. Travis quickly shut the door. He turned his back against it and began panting heavily. This was not real! None of it was real!

He must still be asleep! Anything! He looked around the room for anything that could be used as a weapon. He quickly snatched Katherine's curling iron from the moving box and tightly wrapped his hands around it. He slowly opened the door and looked down both the hallway and staircase.

The house was almost pitch black. This was nothing like their house in Los Angeles. The city lights used to stream through the glass windows and illuminate the entire house. Here, there was barely any visible light but that slipping through the window of the front door.

Travis took another step down the wooden staircase, cautiously squinting into the dark. He pulled his cell phone from his pocket and turned the LED screen on. The dim blue glow barely illuminated two feet in front of him.

A chill ran down his spine as Travis stepped onto the main floor. Even though he didn't want to admit it, this house gave him the chills during the day. Now at night, the house was even creepier. He waved the blue light around as he hesitantly stepped into the darkness.

A patter of steps scurried behind him, making Travis' heart skip a beat. He whirled around as his pulse beat loudly in his ears.

"Hello?" Travis beckoned into the dark. "Show yourself!"

Travis felt his way to the light switch. He flipped the switch but nothing happened. He flipped it again, but the house remained cast in shadows.

"Ethan, is that you?" Travis called. "I'm sorry for what I said earlier."

The sound of a sliding door echoed from somewhere near the basement door. Travis took another deep breath as he tried to calm himself.

"Ethan, come out!" Travis growled as he walked closer to the basement door.

His fingers wrapped around the brass knob. Travis pulled the door open quickly and held the phone in front of him. The glow edged down the steps, stopping just a few stairs from the bottom.

"Ethan are you down ther . . . "Travis stopped as the sound began sliding behind him.

Travis closed his eyes in fear for a moment and forced himself to open them again. He quickly turned to see a thin contorted figure hiding in the dumbwaiter. Before he could fully comprehend what he was seeing, the figure leapt out at him.

Travis jumped backwards and fell down the basement stairs. The door at the top of the stairs slowly began to close. The glow of his cell phone disappeared as the door shut completely. Travis began to panic as he looked around in the darkness.

He groaned as his lower back began to throb with every movement. He began to sit up and realize that almost every part of him was sore and in pain. He wheezed another breath, before forcing himself up.

Suddenly, a slimy object wrapped around Travis's throat. He choked as it began to pull tighter, restricting his breath. Travis grabbed the curling iron from beside him and swung it above his head. It made contact with nothing as the intangible noose began tightening itself.

Travis swung the rod once more with no luck. His feet flailed in every direction as his sweaty hands dropped the iron. He reached for the hands around his throat but could only feel his own hands touching his throat. His left foot unexpectedly caught underneath the bottom stair as he struggled against this relentless force.

With one last ounce of strength, Travis lunged forward with his left leg, pulling himself free from his attacker's resilient grip. Travis quickly scrambled up the staircase and pushed his way through the door. His hands quickly snatched his cell phone from the hardwood floor and turned to find his assailant. He looked down the stairs towards his would-be attacker, but the dim glow kept the basement shrouded in shadows.

Travis shut the basement door and slid the deadbolt. He breathed a sigh of relief as he leaned back against the basement door. As Travis began to take another breath, the sound of feet scuffled in front of him and he snapped the cell phone up.

The cell phone softly illuminated the empty dumbwaiter. He held his breath as he waved the cell phone around. Its blue glow dimly flashed across the wood paneled walls of the foyer.

"Katherine! Call the police!" Travis yelled. "Katherine?!"

Travis stopped as his mouth fell useless. He couldn't believe his eyes. The blue glow of his cell phone harshly illuminated a ghost of his past. Something that could never be real, but yet stood staring directly at him from the living room.

Its dark round eyes stared into Travis' as he found himself unable to speak. The small blonde boy stood alone in the doorway. It was Christian! It was his dead son!

5

Ethan quietly opened the front door as he snuck into the house. He stopped in his tracks as he saw the light of the fireplace flicker from the living room. His eyes narrowed as he slowly shut the door behind him.

Ethan quietly crept across the floor, before stopping to pick up his father's cell phone from the middle of the foyer. He must have dropped it for some reason. He stood up to see his father standing in front of the fireplace, motionless. He stared into the burning embers lost in thought as if he was in a trance.

Ethan shuddered as a cold chill snaked up his spine. His father remained still, gazing into the blazing fire. His shaking hands trembled at his sides as he remained motionless. Ethan slowly began to tiptoe up the stairs as he heard his father mumble something quietly. He stepped back down the stairs as his heart began to race.

Did Travis know? Did his father finally care about him? Ethan's jaw tightened as he waited in anticipation for his father to say something. A tear began to slip down Travis' cheek and slowly slid down the side of his mouth. The tear suspended itself for a moment hanging from his strong chin, before plunging into the ashes. The drop landed atop one of the burning logs and sizzled slowly, before completely evaporating atop the wood.

"I must be losing my mind." Travis muttered quietly, once again.

Ethan held back tears of pain as his father remained ignorant to his presence. The fresh cuts on his forearms stung more than ever, reminding him why he continued his practice. It wasn't just to make himself feel. They were battle scars. Scars formed from the very war he found himself fighting every day.

Ethan dashed up the stairs wiping tears from his dirty cheeks. He found himself in one of the many dark bedrooms and fell atop the antique bed. He buried his face in his pillow and screamed as loud as he could.

He pushed his face deeper into the pillow as each breath began to fade. He gasped as he raised his head and turned over. He wanted to die! What was left in this world? Even Emily would probably find some way to break his heart.

How can people survive in this world? How can they find the want to live? What makes anyone's short, useless lives worth living? Ethan pulled the heavy quilt over himself and sighed. He wiped the tears from his face and stared at the grey ceiling.

Suddenly, Ethan's heart began to pound as the closet doors slowly began to creak open. Ethan's breath began to race as his wide eyes stared fearfully at the dark closet. The dark figure of the shaggy haired man stepped out from his closet only to be silhouetted in the moonlight creeping through the dirty windows. His recognizable form took a step towards Ethan as his wrinkled lips cracked a smile.

Ethan pulled the covers over his head as he forced himself to realize he was dreaming. This isn't happening. This is probably caused by all the stress from his parents and the move. That's right! This is all a self-inflicted hallucination. Ethan was sure a therapist would agree with him.

Yes! Tomorrow morning he would demand that his father arrange for him to see a psychologist. Hopefully they could help him deal with all of these nightmares. Ethan held his breath as he shut his eyes tightly.

He patiently waited for a minute and slowly opened his eyes again. His breath shuddered as he tried to push all negative thoughts from his mind. As his eyes fully opened, the quilt was swiftly torn off of him. The figure's face loomed close to Ethan and paused for a moment. The smell of its alcohol tainted breath wafted into Ethan's face. Its stubbly beard scratched against its wool jacket as the figure's dark, beady eyes watched Ethan closely. The figure watched him with a deadly stare, penetrating deep into Ethan's core. Ethan quickly opened his mouth to scream as the figure's hand quickly shot toward his face.

6

Travis awoke with a startle as his heart skipped a beat. Broken beams of sunlight poured through the dirty windows of the house. He could've sworn those windows were neatly polished the other day. The stress of the move must be getting to him.

He looked at his watch. The hands read five-thirty. He had somehow slept most of the evening. He probably needed it. Maybe Katherine's unwillingness to forgive him of their son's death was finally beginning to weigh on his already heavy heart. Maybe it was just the typical stress of leaving home.

Travis' attention snapped towards the library. An eerie scratching sound scraped along the walls of the den. Travis stood up and cautiously tiptoed towards the source of the noise. The scraping continued as he stepped in the doorway.

A hooded figure snatched at the wallpaper, tearing it from the walls. The mahogany shelves littered the floor as the figure continued its destructive rampage. Travis froze in a moment of panic. Was it the creature from last night? No! That's not possible! He was just exhausted from the move. Is it a burglar?

Travis began searching for a weapon before the figure started to turn its head. Ethan stared coldly at Travis without a word from underneath his red hoodie. His cold grey eyes stared steely at him with a boiling anger, before returning to his work.

"Ethan," Travis began.

Ethan glared at him again, snarling his nose in disgust. Ethan pulled another shelf off the wall, and tossed it onto the pile of broken boards before tearing off a new piece of wallpaper.

"What are you doing?" Travis cried. "Ethan?! Answer me!"

Ethan continued to ignore his father's calls as he hastily tore apart the library. He reached for another board and threw it behind himself, narrowly missing Travis. Travis flinched as the board slammed against the matching French doors behind him.

"Ethan!" Travis growled angrily, before sighing in defeat.

Travis took another step back and closed the study's doors. He ran his fingers through his messy hair and shook his head in frustration. He quickly sprinted up the staircase and knocked on the door of the master bedroom. There was no answer. He knocked again before slowly opening the creaking door.

Travis sighed as another board slammed against the hardwood floor downstairs. Travis shut the bedroom door behind him causing the sounds of Ethan's rampage to become muffled.

The sight of Katherine's sleeping face calmed Travis as his concern for her last night overcame his thoughts and washed away his troubles with Ethan.

There was something about her gentle body lying among the tossed covers that made her seem almost angelic. It stirred up the excitement he had when he first asked her out in those cold, winter months inside that warm coffee shop. Travis quietly walked over and sat on the bed.

He silently slipped off his shoes and stretched out on the massive king-size bed. He looked at Katherine's pale complexion and smiled. This was his wife. This was the woman he loved. Nothing could come between that.

She blinked her green eyes open and stared at him. He felt as if they were almost smiling as their emerald gaze bored deep into his soul. Her mouth slowly moved closer to him and paused close to his lips. He swallowed in anticipation as his heart began to race.

Was this truly what she wanted? What had made her change her mind? Had she finally forgiven him? Travis pulled away in consideration. She had been so angry with him for so long, why would she be any different now? Why did they both see Christian last night?

He sat up and turned to sit on the edge of the uncomfortably firm bed. He stared at the old wooden floorboards as he became lost in thought.

"I'm sorry," Travis managed as a tear slipped down his chiseled cheek. "I don't know what else I could've done."

He turned to see Katherine staring at him without any visible emotion. He returned to examining the floorboards. His chest began to pull from inside of him as his heart constricted in pain.

"I know you were watching him, but . . . but you were afraid of the water."

Travis paused for a moment and wiped away another tear before continuing.

"If I had told Adriana to use the study hall or some other learning resource center, maybe I would have walked back outside earlier. If I had just hung up the phone . . ."

Travis swallowed another hard lump in his throat. He needed to explain. He needed to get everything out in the open. Not only for her sake, but this was for his own good. He needed to release everything he had been bottling up for the last year.

"But no! I told her I'd meet her at my office to help her with her homework. I should've known something was off. I should've recognized the signs. Maybe I did. I just didn't want to believe them."

"That's when I heard you yelling. Screaming - at the top of your lungs. I ran outside to see you, magazine in hand staring into the pool. I saw Christian lying motionless in the bottom of the pool. He struggled for one last breath before I could even do anything."

"I jumped in as quickly as I could. I did. I really did. But that was no use. It was all no use. I pulled his body to the surface, but . . ."

"You didn't see how pale he was. Lying on the bottom of the pool. His body was curled up so tightly. He was so cold. So . . . freezing cold."

"When I pulled him to the surface, his body finally fell limp. You dragged him onto the patio and rested his head against the concrete ground. I tried giving him air, but he wouldn't take any of it. He was already gone."

"How long was it? How long was it until you noticed that he was drowning? Were you reading? Were you so absorbed in keeping a distance from the family, that you couldn't even pay attention to your own son? How long was it until you noticed him missing? Until you noticed that your own ignorance killed our son?!"

Travis stood up and stared angrily at her. "I know it was my fault as well, but couldn't you have done something?"

Travis walked over to the bathroom and rested his head against the closed door. Katherine sat up and slowly slid herself off of the bed. She walked over to him and softly touched his cheek.

"I love you so much." Travis cried. "And I love Christian. I love Ethan. But maybe we've been ignoring each other too much. Maybe we've pushed each other away, when we should've been becoming a family."

Katherine moved closer and kissed Travis gingerly. She pulled away slowly while staring into his brown eyes. Another tear streamed down his cheek and slid against her hand.

"I buried myself in my work and you came and saw Adriana approach me. You stopped in that parking lot and watched as she tried to kiss me. You walked away as I told her that I would never, ever do anything like that. She's a child for goodness sake!"

"She's someone else's child! She's someone else's child and she's falling. She's falling deeper and deeper into that dark water. And she's drowning in her own self-worthlessness. She's practically selling herself! But I can't save her. I can't ever save any of them!"

"Christian. Adriana. Who's next? Who am I going to have to watch slip into that darkness and fall away from me? How many more will I lose? Because of my own mistakes, they just fall further and further. Can't I reach someone in time? Can't I save them? Why can't I ever save them?"

Travis began to turn the bathroom door's knob, before Katherine's cold hand rested atop of his.

"This is good." She nodded gently and looked back up at him. "I don't want to remember last night, though. Please don't make me relive that. You're right we need to move on."

Travis' hand slipped from the doorknob and smoothly slid around her waist. He rested his head against hers and stared into her beautiful eyes.

"I forgive you." Travis tightened his lips and forced back another tear. "Even though all that has happened – I forgive you.

And I'm sorry. I'm so sorry. I'm so sorry for everything. Will you ever be able to forgive me?"

Katherine pulled away from him and walked over to one of the cardboard boxes. Travis watched her in hope as she remained silent. She stared into what seemed like a bottomless box and sighed. There was no answer. She could never forgive him of that incident. She *would* never forgive him. Travis lowered his head in disappointment.

Ethan tossed another board to the ground and sighed. His fingers found another wrinkled edge and tore back one of the last pieces of wallpaper.

"I love what you've done with the place!" Emily squeaked sarcastically as she hopped over one of the antique shelves.

Ethan glared at her in frustration, before turning back to the wall to admire his work.

"What's the matter? Cat got your tongue?" Emily teased as she successfully made her way over to him.

She turned to look at the mural Ethan had uncovered. It was a strange circle subdivided into seven pie shaped sections. Each section had its own uniquely gruesome etching. They were reminiscent to the early sketches found in medieval texts and tomes. In the center of the round mural was a smaller circle. Inside this small circle was another drawing.

"Fascinating isn't it?" Emily grinned as she admired each grisly scrawl. "It's said that the pictures bordering the larger circle are representations of the seven deadly sins."

Ethan's eyes narrowed at her as she began to explain each illustration.

"Gluttony." She pointed to the depiction of an over-sized naked woman feeding her face with mouthfuls of fruit. It's the over-indulgence of anything. You name it. Food, objects, etcetera."

She waved her finger to the next painting. It was of a mousy looking man with a grin that literally stretched from ear to ear. His arms wrapped around several stacks of coins atop a table. "Greed. Similarly a sin of excess, but it deals more with the focus of material items. But, I think you understand this one."

"Moving on," the next picture was of a wormy looking naked man lying atop a puddle of mud. "Sloth is a laziness that can sometimes include the spiritual. Some even say it's when people ignore the grace given to them."

"Wrath and envy," She pointed to two separate pictures.

One was of a woman standing atop a man with a dagger plunged in between his eyes. The other was of a man's eyes burning in lust as he watched a woman bathe from a distance.

"These are relatable, but completely different. Wrath can be an anger directed towards someone or something. Murder, revenge and even suicide can be a sin of anger directed inwardly."

Ethan tightened his jaw as he stared at the energetic redhead. She knew so much about this, but yet she remained unwilling to compromise the mystery surrounding her. He didn't know if he was in love with her or if he was just utterly confused.

"Ever heard of the command: Thou shalt not covet anything of your neighbor's? Well that pretty much sums up envy. Even King David was guilty of becoming envious of Bathsheba's husband as he longed for her. He was so envious that he had him placed on the front lines of his army, just so he could make Bathsheba his wife."

"Next, lust." She smiled and stepped even closer to Ethan. Her eyes smiled up at him, before returning to explaining the illustrations. The picture was of naked man pressing an equally naked woman against a tree and kissing her neck. "The intense desire of something, whether it be sex, money, fame, or any other object of passion."

Ethan shook his head slightly and took a step away from a very close Emily. Her arm gently brushed against his as she smiled teasingly. Ethan sneered and took another step away.

"Finally, pride." This was a very disconcerting picture as the figure was depicted as screaming in agony. Their excruciating pain was being caused by horrible, disfigured creatures tearing the woman's stomach apart and crawling out from inside of it. "This is considered to be the worst of them all. Pride is the love of your own being. It is the intense desire of yourself and only yourself. Pride can be expressed in many ways and has been depicted any many ways. If only the person would show a shred of humility would things be different, but most are obsessed with their concerns only."

Ethan pointed to the circular picture in the middle. He stared at Emily intently as his lips tightened.

"Okay," Emily shrugged. "The center picture is more of the owner's son's addition. It's not a sin, but it depicts more of an inflicted punishment."

The sketch was of a man gasping in fear as he encounters his dead body on the ground. His pale corpse lied on the ground with a sword driven through his heart. Blood flowed from the wound and created a large paddle amassing his entire body. The grass around the body was violently drawn as being depicted of dying and tuning completely black. A dark spectral figure is shown trailing from the body's mouth to the living person. The person's eyes are now a dark black as the figure seeps into his eyes. Tormented faces are illustrated behind him emerging from the walls. Their faces scream in terror and laughter as they move closer to escaping their confinement and reaching their prey.

"From what I've heard it was supposed to be about death. Once the person died on this special "dead" ground, they would still walk amongst the living. They are still themselves and can do whatever they please, until they discover their dead corpse."

"After learning that they have died, the darkness of their place of death consumes them. The dead are then cursed to be trapped in their surroundings. None of their original being remains except in appearance. The darkness can use their memories as a sort of camouflage as they hunt their next victims. They feed off of the darkness inside of people. That's how they gain power. They typically prey on people that are utterly consumed in the darkness as they provide less of a fight."

Ethan's eyes narrowed again. Emily was beginning to scare him. Now that he knew these drawings were in the house, he was becoming even more uncomfortable with staying here.

"Ethan!" Travis called from atop the staircase.

"Well, that's my cue to leave." Emily smiled as she dashed over to the window.

Ethan turned to grab her, but she was already halfway out the opening.

"See ya later?" Emily grinned as Ethan nodded in confirmation. "Cool!"

The titian-haired girl closed the window silently, before waving goodbye. Her bright eyes locked onto Travis as he shuffled down the staircase inside the house. Her red hair whipped around as she darted into the shrubbery and quickly disappeared.

Ethan continued to stare after her as he felt his father's strong hand rest on his shoulder. Ethan turned to look his father in the eyes.

"Ethan, I'm sorry about earlier." Travis apologized. "If you have something to say about this house than I'll listen."

Ethan felt himself wanting to cry inside. He wanted to tell his father about all the weird things he had seen in this house. He wanted to tell him about the man on the top of the stairs and what he had done to him last night. He wanted to explain how he couldn't move when they first explored the house as his legs had become uncontrollably frozen. More than anything, he wanted to tell him about Emily. But all of these were impossible.

7

Ethan couldn't say a word. His mouth was sealed shut and so was anything inside of it. Anything that Ethan wanted to say now, he couldn't. Ethan looked over at the broken mirror on the library wall. The reflection showed his horrifying lipless face again. There was no opening. His mouth was melted shut and he could not open it.

He had tried a knife this morning, but could still feel his lips on his face. Whatever this was, his lips were still physically on his face. Other people that were talking to him weren't noticing they were missing. Was this all just a part of his imagination? Or was something supernatural impairing him from speaking?

"Well, if you do want to speak to me," Travis smiled. "That's fine. Just know that I'm here."

Travis patted Ethan once more on the shoulder and left the library. Ethan stood amongst the piles of shelves and wallpaper as Travis' footsteps pattered across the foyer. An icy chill quickly shot up Ethan's spine as he began to gather his thoughts.

How could he communicate? Why was this man attacking him? Who was he? Was he even real? Ethan stared into the mirror and inspected his mouth. He ran his fingers along his lips and could feel their soft touch. He tried stretching his mouth as far as he could but his fingers revealed his mouth was unmoving.

Ethan looked down and pulled his blade from his back pocket. He pulled it out of the black case and sighed. Shadows fell across the room as if the sky had become overcast. Ethan looked back up and his heart skipped a beat as the mirror reflected the familiar haggard-looking figure standing behind him.

A loud knock rapped against the front door and quickly pulled Travis from the kitchen. He briskly strolled over to the heavy wooden door and peered out the stained glass window. It was their real estate agent, Evelyn. Travis sighed in disgust and opened the door.

"Good morning to you Mr. Holloway!" She exclaimed as she slipped her way into the house. "How's the new house treating you?"

"Uh. Fine, I guess. Come on in." Travis murmured reluctantly.

"Good. Good. So you're settling in alright?" She grinned while inspecting the foyer.

"Yeah. Everything's fine." Travis stared at the aging woman inquisitively. "I hope you don't mind me asking, but what are you doing here?"

"Oh." Evelyn crinkled her nose and smiled. "I usually come to check on my client's the day after their 'big move.'" She motioned captioning the phrase in the air.

"Oook." Travis raised his eyebrow. "We're all good here. Thanks for dropping by."

"Oh, now don't be rude Mr. Holloway." Evelyn pinched his arm playfully and began walking towards the living room. "At least offer me a drink before I leave."

"Alright." Travis frowned in confusion. At this point he just wanted her to leave. "What would you like? We've got water, tea . . . I think there might be a can of soda in one of the boxes."

"No, no, no. I'm talking about the good stuff." The greying agent bent down and pulled a bottle of aged cognac from one of the lower cabinets of the bookshelves. She held up the bottle proudly and pulled two glasses from the cabinet.

"How did you?" Travis began, before being cut off in mid-sentence by the pushy lady.

"It's my job. As the real estate agent, I know every inch of these houses." She smiled warmly and poured them both a drink.

Evelyn walked the bottle over to Travis and pushed a cup into his hand. "To your family. May you and they be happy in this humble abode for a very long time."

Travis hesitantly tapped glasses with the sour-faced agent and then raised the cup to his lips. He forced the drink down roughly as the swig burnt against the walls of his throat. He painfully sighed and winced at the strong aftertaste.

"Ah! Like I said; the good stuff." Ms. Wiles smiled joyfully, before sitting in one of the large oak chairs. "You know some owners never make it a day in these new houses,"

Travis growled in frustration as he sat in an adjacent matching chair. Evelyn's tired eyes began staring at the empty fireplace and became lost in thought. She took another sip of the cognac and closed her eyes.

"What do you mean?" Travis asked, anxious to get rid of his unwanted visitor.

"Some find their new houses to be too much for them." She opened her eyes again, staring ahead at the cold coals and ashes resting inside the fireplace. "A new place is intimidating and sometimes . . . sometimes it just overwhelms the new owners."

Evelyn sighed in meditation. She finished her drink and set it on the oak coffee table. "Thank you for the drink. I'll show myself out."

Ms. Wiles stood up and brushed off her dress. She shook Travis' hand and smiled once again. "I apologize for my intrusion."

Nodding to Travis, she walked back into the foyer. Travis watched her leave the room and turned back to staring at the burnt-out coals. "That was weird," he thought as he looked at Evelyn's half–drank glass of cognac.

He picked the glass up and inspected it. A sticky black residue was smeared on the outside of the rim. He brushed his finger over the stain. Immediately, the dark residue stuck to his finger. He pulled his finger up from the cup and watched as it stretched like bubble gum. Travis frowned as he set the sticky glass back down.

In the hall, Evelyn brushed her hand along the wood-paneled walls before coming to a rest against the library door. She gently pushed it open to see Ethan standing in front of the mirror. He turned to look at her and gave her a menacing stare.

"Careful, now. Jasper's been known to bite." Evelyn smiled darkly, before turning to leave.

She waved her hand and Ethan's eyes began to widen. Black puncture wounds riddled her fingertips. Ethan dashed out of the library and slid to a halt. He firmly grabbed Evelyn's shoulder and turned her around.

He gasped for all he could, instead inhaling a deep breath. Rather than Evelyn's old, wrinkled face, Emily's youthful appearance turned to look him in the eyes. She was dressed in Evelyn's outdated pink dress and hideous open-toed shoes.

8

"Very good, champ!" Emily punched his shoulder with youthful excitement. "You finally figured it out. It's been like, what? A day?"

Ethan's lips tightened as he stared coldly into Emily's eyes. Who was she? Was she Evelyn? Was she Emily?

Emily pulled her shoulder out of his hard grip and smiled. She trotted to the door and slung it open. Turning back, Emily smiled and blew Ethan an imaginary kiss. "Just know this. You're only beginning to scratch the surface. . . . See ya later?"

Emily flashed her eyes at him energetically and closed the door behind herself. Ethan stood paralyzed in the foyer. His heart raced as his mind struggled to keep up. This was so far outside of his league. This is like the stuff you would see in movies or television. Real life isn't like this! People can't just change into other people!

An idea flashed inside of Ethan's mind. He ran back into the library and returned with a notepad and pencil. Shadows began to fall outside of the house and the entire house began to darken with nightfall. Ethan ran into the living room and poked Travis' shoulder.

"What is it?" Travis scooted to the edge of the chair, pulling himself from its deep seat. "You need something?"

Ethan shook his head in frustration and quickly jotted something down on the notepad. He turned the pad around so his father could read it.

"Can't speak!" Travis read aloud in a hushed tone. "What do you mean? You want to go somewhere else? Is it your mom?"

Ethan shook his head again and tore off the top sheet. He scribbled another note and held it up for his father to see.

"Can't move my mouth!" Travis laughed. "What are you talking about? Of course you can! If this is another ploy for attention . . ."

Travis stopped as he saw the fear in Ethan's eyes. This was his last hope. He needed his father to believe him. Travis nodded his head and agreed to play along. "Okay. Okay. You can't speak. What do you want to tell me?"

Ethan paused for a moment and then scribbled another message on the next page. He took a moment and looked at the note before turning it over.

It read: THIS HOUSE IS EVIL!!!!!!!!!!!!

Travis stifled a laugh and looked for his son to crack a smile. When a smile did not come, Travis took another deep breath and continued to play along. "Why? Why is this house evil?"

Ethan quickly scratched another note into the yellowing pad of paper. Travis tapped his foot impatiently as he looked up at his son. Ethan flipped the paper around and held his message out with a shaky hand.

"A man came into my room and took my voice." Travis frowned. "What man? How could he take your voice?"

Travis looked back up at his son and stopped. Ethan's eyes were wide with fear. He swallowed deeply and raised his hand. He pointed behind Travis and held his trembling arm aloft in the air. Travis turned to see a dirty looking man standing before the front door.

Travis's heart began to pound loudly in his ears as he slowly stood up. "Travis stay here," he instructed as he stood all the way up. He cautiously grabbed a fire poker from beside the fireplace and moved forward.

"Who are you?" Travis called to the man. "What do you want?"

The man remained silent as he was still. His long hair covered the majority of his face as his dark eyes watched the father and son from underneath his eyebrows. His stubbly beard was stained with a sticky crimson substance as he smiled tauntingly. His ragged clothes looked like antiques and were stained with years of mud.

"What do you want?!" Travis screamed as he edged closer.

A scream from the upper floor echoed throughout the foyer. Travis paused in his tracks and looked towards the master bedroom. Katherine!

"Ethan! Upstairs now!" Travis said as the man began slowly walking towards him. "Now!"

Travis' heart began skipping a beat as the man's walk became a full-out sprint. Travis and Ethan dashed up the stairs. The sun had set quicker than they had realized and the house was beginning to be consumed in shadows. The beams of sunlight through the muddy windows were no more and only the dark of night remained.

Ethan and Travis tripped up the stairs as they raced for safety. Ethan's right foot caught a hold of a stair's lip and tossed him forward against the staircase. He turned to look back at his attacker as his hands fumbled for the ground behind him. He began scrambling up the stairs backwards, when he felt a hand

grab his hoodie.

9

Ethan turned to see a decaying hand reaching out of the wall, tightly gripping his hoodie sleeve. The first hand was soon joined by other hands snapping out of the wall towards him. Faces began pushing themselves out of the walls as the wall stretched across their widening mouths. Their decrepit faces moaned as they shoved their way forward.

Ethan tried to scream, but couldn't. Travis grabbed his arm as Ethan slipped the hoodie off from around himself. Travis pulled his son safely to the top of the stairs as he stared in horror at the sight before his eyes. Ethan kicked another snapping hand from off of his leg as his father turned his attention to Katherine.

Travis shook the knob to the master bedroom as Ethan panted in fright. He looked down the staircase to see the hands and faces part for the shaggy-haired man. His heart pounded as he saw the numerous appendages driving themselves out from the walls.

"Katherine!" Travis yelled as he pounded his fist against the locked door. "Katherine!"

Travis took a step back and kicked the door in. The door swung inwards on its hinges and slammed against the wall. Travis rushed into the room and wrapped his arms around Katherine.

He held her tight as the sounds of the horrors began to creep closer.

"What's going on?" Katherine asked as she looked at the two panting for breath.

Ethan closed the door behind him and gasped for air as he leaned against it. His eyes caught sight of a wooden dresser on the opposite side of the room. He pushed himself away from the door and ran towards the high-boy. He shot a pained glance at his father as he struggled to drag the dresser across the room.

Travis quickly grabbed the opposite side of the cabinet and helped push the heavy dresser against the door. The men backed up a few steps as a barrage of fists began pounding on the door outside.

"There's too many! That won't hold for long!" Travis exclaimed as he backed up towards the bathroom.

Ethan grabbed his startled mother and began dragging her to the bathroom. Katherine dug her heels into the ground as she shook her head vehemently. Travis ran over to Katherine and put a reassuring hand on her shoulder.

"C'mon! Honey, you'll be fine." Travis grabbed her hand and gave her a comforting smile.

"No! I can't!" She screamed. "I can't go in there!"

Ethan pounded on the bathroom door behind his father as Travis tried dragging Katherine along. "Yeah, I know!" Travis waived Ethan off as he tried to comfort Katherine. "Now please. You can do this for me."

Travis looked deep into her green eyes and nodded. "I know you can."

Ethan pounded on the door again and Travis spun around angrily. "Yeah? What?!" he exclaimed as his son, pointed into the bathroom. Travis took one more step and looked inside the brightly-lit bathroom before his heart stopped beating for a moment. Water oozed across the white-tiled floor and into the master bedroom. Travis trembled as the water seeped through his shoes and soaked into his socks.

Inside the bathroom Katherine lied motionless in the bathtub. Her pale body was submerged in the overflowing tub. Her face was swollen and showed signs of pruned wrinkles. She had been underwater for a very long time. Travis forced back tears as he turned back to the Katherine he so desperately clung to.

Dark particles floated inside her eyes before collecting together into a reflective black oil substance. The dark substance dripped down her cheeks as her mouth opened to reveal several rows of razor sharp teeth. The kind of teeth that reminded him of those he had only seen on sharks before.

"I told you not to go in there." The dark-eyed Katherine hissed.

Ethan grabbed his father's shoulder and pulled him into the bathroom. He quickly locked the door behind them as Travis fell to his knees in tears. His father pulled Katherine's body from the tub and held her close. He cradled her shoulders in his arms as he set his forehead on hers. His body shook hysterically as her wet forehead pressed against his.

Ethan grabbed the shower curtain and tossed it over his mother's exposed body. His throat began to constrict as he watched his father weep over his dead mother. Travis pulled the curtain over her shoulders as he rocked her body.

"She was drowning last night." Travis stammered. "But I saved her. I saved her and laid her in bed."

Ethan jumped as a coat rod slammed through the bathroom door, narrowly missing his head. Ethan knelt down and shook his father's shoulder urgently. Travis nodded as he continued to sob.

Ethan looked into his father's eyes and pleaded with his father for help using only stares.

Travis kissed his wife's lips once more before setting Katherine's cold body against the cold tile floor. "I love you, honey . . . I'm so sorry I failed you." He stood up, wiping the tears from his face as Ethan tried pushing the window open. Travis took one last look at his departed wife. The coat rod slammed through the bathroom door again, this time creating a wider crack in the door.

The evil Katherine's beady black eyes stared into the room like a predator stalking her prey. Her head cocked to the side unnaturally as she watched the two men. Ethan turned to see her face disappear from the small crack and continue driving the dowel rod through the door. Behind the Katherine impostor, he could see the dresser fall to the floor. The creatures pushed through the splinters of what used to be the master bedroom door, hissing in excitement. They appeared to be slender humanoid figures, disfigured and anorexic. Their indistinguishable dark bodies climbed over one another as they broke inside. Their elongated mouths snapped like piranhas as they moved closer.

Ethan turned back and both of them slammed the window up. Travis pushed Ethan to crawl out first and quickly followed. The horde could be heard clamoring through the master bedroom and beginning to break through the bathroom door.

"We can't jump from here." Travis noted as he stared down at the ground. "We'd never make it."

The two stood side by side hugging the walls of the house, while standing on a narrow ledge. Ethan looked down and nodded in agreement.

"Let's try the far bedroom," Travis motioned towards the corner of the house. "Maybe we can slip back in and make it to the ground floor."

Ethan carefully shuffled across the ledge, being sure to keep most of his weight on his toes. The narrow ledge could be felt cracking underneath their weight. Ethan closed in on the window and stopped. He looked inside the room to make sure there weren't any creatures waiting to pounce on them in hunger.

His fingers searched for the bottom of the window and wrapped themselves around it. He pulled up, but the window stopped as grout jammed the window from sliding. He rattled the window again, but it was impossibly stuck. Ethan snorted in frustration as he looked back at his dad.

"What? What is it?" Travis asked, quickly looking back towards the bathroom window. "Can we get in?"

Ethan sighed and pulled the black case from his back pocket. Travis' eyes widened as he watched his son pull the blood-stained razor blade from the case. Ethan's eyes began to tear up as he realized what his father must be thinking.

"Ethan." His father exclaimed sadly as he looked at him.

Ethan turned in shame as he began to use the razor blade to dig the grout from the slides. Travis grabbed Ethan's forearm. He winced in pain as his father's fingers wrapped around his scars. Travis pulled his son's shirt sleeve up enough to see the rows of self-inflicted scars he had collected over time.

"Ethan." His dad's voice cracked. "Why?"

Ethan sniffled and dug the grout out quicker. The window fell against the sill as the mechanism was cleared. Ethan blinked tears away as he forced himself to focus on the matter at hand. He pulled the window up and checked inside again.

He nodded towards his father and quickly climbed inside. The sounds of the creepers could be heard down the hall. Their slimy sneers slithered over each other's angered hisses. Travis scrambled in and pulled himself the rest of the way through. Ethan held a finger to his lips as he shot a glance at his father.

Travis nodded in affirmation and quietly walked to the door.

Slowly, he peered around the doorframe and watched as a crowd of hulking creepers pushed into the bedroom. Ethan gasped silently as he noticed the baby's crib in the corner of the room. That thing had always given him the creeps before and it was certainly doing the same right now.

"Are you ready?" Travis' tear filled eyes stared wearily at Ethan.

Ethan wiped the tears from his father's eyes with his shirt sleeve and nodded. Travis smiled bleakly and took a deep breath. He waved for Ethan to follow him as they poised to dash across the hall. Without warning, a baby's cry sounded from the crib. Ethan and Travis gasped as they heard the creepers take notice of the sound.

10

Ethan cursed silently at the crib. They both quickly acknowledged the need to flee their position and tore down the hall. Ethan followed his father as they shuffled down the stairs. The scuffling of the creatures behind them began to increase in sound as they reached the ground floor.

Travis ran to the front door and tried to pull it open. The door knob was frozen in position. He shook the knob again, but the door was completely locked. Travis tried to turn the deadbolt, but an unknown force held the lock in place.

Ethan fumbled in the dark, searching for the light switch. His hand ran across it and he flipped the toggle. Nothing happened. The whole house had seemed to go dark with the fall of night and everything appeared to be dead.

"I can't see anything in this dark!" Travis grumbled as he gave up on the front door.

The creatures were already halfway down the staircase and Ethan's breathing became even shorter. Travis smacked Ethan on the back and led him towards the study. Ethan tripped into the coffee table and heard a glass smash against the hardwood floor. Travis grabbed a box of matches and quickly lit one in order to navigate the dark halls of the house.

Ethan pointed towards the back door as the creepers began to close in on them. Travis nodded and winced as the flame singed his fingertips. He dropped the match and pulled Ethan into the kitchen. Ethan turned back as the creepers began to squeal. The match had landed on the spilt remains of cognac and lit the puddle ablaze. The creepers hissed as they scurried around the flame, making sure to stay in the shadows.

Travis tugged at Ethan's arm and pulled him into the kitchen. He tried the locks to the back door with the same result as the front door. The door was locked solid and remained immovable. Ethan patted his dad's shoulder and took a few steps back. He took a run at the glass door and busted the pane. Ethan backed up again and they both threw their weight into the door. The glass shattered and they fell atop the shards on the back porch.

Ethan groaned as he rolled over in the shards. Travis picked him up and motioned towards the front gates. Ethan nodded and they both tore across the lawn. The creepers could be heard moving along the shadowed walls of the estate. Their jaws snapped like hungry crocodiles chasing after their next meal.

Ethan reached the gate first and fumbled with the lock. Travis snatched the lock from his hands and quickly flipped through the numbers. Ethan's heart raced as he could see crowds of monstrous human shapes running alongside the shadowy walls. Their eyes were as black as oil and reminded him of Emily's blood. She was one of them! She was an evil being of some sort.

"There!" Travis exclaimed as the lock sprung open. He swung the wrought-iron gate against the stone wall and pushed Ethan through. The monsters were right behind them. He took one last look at the house in memory of Katherine. He would come back here in the light with an army of cops and retrieve Katherine's body. He would give her a proper burial. She didn't deserve to die in a nightmare like that house.

11

Ethan shuddered as the world around him had changed. He didn't know what had happened. He was just outside with his father and now he was surrounded in pitch black. He couldn't see anything as he moved around, feeling for anything tangible.

Objects brushed against his hands. They were soft and felt like wool. He ran his hands up and down them trying to understand their shape. They felt like coats. Nice, wool dress coats of some sort. Where was he? What had happened?

A cold chill began to run up his spine as he felt a peeling hand wrap around his mouth. Another hand began to grab his ankle and another grabbed his throat. Their grip began to constrict and grow even tighter. Ethan flailed his arms about, searching for an escape. He tore at the hand around his mouth as his breath began to shorten.

His hands found a solid wall in front of him and he began to pound on the wall violently. He pounded again and again, hoping to break the wall. The hands began to pull him backwards into the dark abyss. Ethan wrestled against their strong grip and pounded on the wall again.

The wall swung open and Travis grabbed Ethan's right hand. Ethan shook the hands off of his legs and scratched at the hand around his throat. He grabbed the fingers and pulled them backwards. They were boneless. Their fingers could be bent in any direction and they would not break.

Travis pulled him the rest of the way out of the darkness and slammed the closet door behind Ethan. Ethan panted as he stared at the closed closet door. What was that? Why were they back in the house?

"We can't leave." Travis moaned, putting his hands on his head. "I turned to see you were gone. I took one step outside those walls and found myself in the library."

"Oh, s . . !" Travis began hyperventilating. "We can't leave. We can't escape them."

The creepers could be heard running across the lawn. Their loud snapping sounds and whispers made Ethan's hands tremble with fear. He searched his mind for any possible escape. Anything! His eyes darted around the foyer, before catching sight of something of interest. The dumbwaiter!

If they couldn't escape the creatures, maybe they could wait them out. Ethan pointed towards the large dumbwaiter. He pushed past his father and opened the door. He motioned inside the shaft.

"No! Not in there! I can't!" Travis shook his head aggressively.

Ethan shoved his father forward. He felt inside for the pulley and lowered the lift another foot, in order to stand inside the shaft. Travis reluctantly crawled atop the platform and Ethan quickly followed. Ethan slid the door closed behind them. They both held their breaths in fear as the creepers could be heard scurrying through the halls.

Ethan pointed towards his father and held his finger up to his lips. Travis closed his eyes and exhaled. The sounds of the creepers began to separate throughout the house. Through the cracks of the wooden door, Ethan could see the empty hallway.

Ethan began to relax as the hallway seemed to be empty. Suddenly a creeper's face appeared in front of the door. Its dark eyes stared into Ethan's as its mouth widened into a smile. Ethan held his breath trying his best to keep from gasping. He noticed Travis had been holding his breath for a while. Ethan stood back up and motioned for him to exhale. Travis let out a single breath and lost it immediately.

12

The lift cracked under their weight and plummeted another story. Ethan fell on top of Travis and heard a snap. Travis screamed in pain as Ethan stood atop Travis' leg. Ethan hurried off of his leg and slid open the dumbwaiter door.

He climbed out onto the cold floor of the dingy basement. Moonlight illuminated the dark basement from a small window on the far side of the room. Travis muffled a moan as Ethan pulled him from the chute. Ethan felt his leg for any broken bones. Travis winced as he pulled himself onto his feet. The good thing was it wasn't broken. At most his ankle was just sprained. But how long could he keep running on it?

Ethan darted up the steps and locked the door. He could hear the creepers racing down the stairs towards the sound of the broken dumbwaiter. Ethan returned to his father, who was now scouring the shelves for any weapons of use.

"Did you notice how they avoided the fire?" Travis noted, "I don't think it wasn't the fire they were avoiding. I think it was the light."

"Maybe that's why they have to stay in the shadows outside." Travis explained.

Ethan thought of Evelyn showing them the house. That was

in the afternoon, but Travis did pose an interesting point. Maybe Evelyn or Emily is a special kind of these creatures. Maybe some *can* be seen in the light.

Travis grabbed a few dirty rags and a bottle of oil. Ethan grabbed several Mason jars and a flashlight from a degrading cardboard box. He brought them over to Travis as he began soaking the rags in the oil. Ethan checked the batteries in the flashlight and turned it on.

The beam of light swept across the room illuminating the grimy grey walls. The light snapped to the top of the stairs as the creepers began pounding on the basement door. Travis pulled the box of matches from his pocket and readied himself.

"Ethan," Travis said, looking up at his son. "I know I haven't been there for you until now. But . . . I'll get us out of this."

Ethan watched as Travis' eyes began to swell up with tears. "I'm sorry you felt you had to do the things you did." Travis pointed towards his son's arm. "I should've been a better father. Your mother . . ."

"Your mother and I had our differences." Travis choked as he watched the top of the stairs. "But we love you. We're proud of the man you've become."

Ethan's eyes narrowed as his ears began to feel warm. The creepers scratched at the door as Ethan watched his father's eyes redden.

"But I've lost so many people." Travis calmed himself as he stared at the ground. "Your mother. Christian. I won't lose you, too."

Ethan rested his hand atop his father's shoulder and looked him confidently in the eyes. Travis nodded in understanding and swallowed again. "I won't lose you. I won't. I'll protect you."

Ethan nodded understandingly. A crack sounded from the top of the stairs as the creepers began breaking through. One of their hands slipped through the crack and grasped for anything within reach.

"Ready?" Travis asked as he stood up, regaining his composure.

Ethan nodded and faked a smile for his father. Travis appreciated the sincerity and grabbed one of the jars. He took out the match from the box and struck it against a nearby support beam. He held the match above the Mason jar momentarily, before dropping it atop the oily rags.

The rag quickly caught ablaze and burned bright. Travis

stared at the captured flame for a second before hurling it up the stairs. The jar shattered against the basement door. The flames quickly crept up the bottom of the door and began to engulf the stairwell in flames.

The creepers screams could be heard from behind the closed doors. The hand that had been reaching through the door was now aflame and flailing back and forth in pain. The creature pulled its arm from the door and the creepers could be heard screeching at the light.

Travis tossed another jar up the stairs, adding to the rapidly growing fire. The flames licked at the doorknob and reminded Ethan of the melted door jam. His mind raced with confusion as his heart beat faster and faster.

"Ethan?" Travis pointed towards a trapdoor in the basement floor.

Ethan's flashlight beam unknowingly was trained on the wood panel and caught Travis' eye. Its sturdy iron handle was easily as old as the house itself. The solid construction gave them hope that whatever was beneath the door, might keep them from becoming the creeper's next meal. Or at the very least delay the inevitable.

Ethan dashed over to the hatch and pulled at the handle. The metal grip snapped from its place with old age. Ethan tossed it across the basement floor and dug his fingers underneath the aging boards. Travis grabbed a crowbar and slid it underneath one of the panels.

He strained against the door as the blood vessels in his forehead flared. Ethan grabbed the bottom of the crowbar and pulled with his father. The boards began to creak and snap with a splintering crack.

Ethan stood back and watched the burning staircase. Travis pried the first board up and wrapped his hands around the surrounding boards. The door to the staircase snapped in half as creepers began pushing their way through. They shrieked as they crawled over the flames.

Travis heaved backwards and pulled another board from its jammed position. Ethan snapped his flashlight up the stairs and trained it on the incoming horde. They cried out in pain as their black skin reddened like coals. Their flesh became like charcoal and illuminated with a red hot blaze, before exploding in ashes.

One creeper charged towards Ethan in a Hail-Mary attempt for the others. Ethan stumbled backwards as he trained the flashlight beam into its chest. The creeper took another step forward and stopped inches from Ethan's face.

Corvus Winchester

13

The creeper growled as its upper lip flinched in disgust. Its black eyes began to redden with heat. Ethan could feel the warmth singe his face as he stared into its menacing eyes. The creeper's skin brightened with intensity before exploding in a cloud of dust. Ethan coughed as he waved the ashes away from his face.

Ethan's eyes widened as he realized the power of his tool. His mouth crept into a smile as he waved the beam back and forth. The creatures screamed in pain as the beam tunneled into their bodies, causing them to explode.

"Ethan! Come on!" Travis called, waving him over to the open passageway.

Ethan slowly backed up and waited till his father slipped through. He tossed the flashlight down to his father and grabbed another Mason jar. He lit the Mason jar on fire and tossed it towards the top of the stairs. He could at least try to slow the creatures down while they tried to figure out their next move.

The jar broke before the foot of a creeper and immersed his body in flames. The creeper shrieked as its body burned before its eyes. It quickly charged down the stairs, running straight for its attacker. Ethan scrambled over to the hatch and squeezed himself into the hole. The creeper tripped over the box of Mason jars and lit the entire box aflame.

The oil-covered rags caught ablaze and began to burn. Several more creepers clambered down the stairs, smashing the glass jars. The fire quickly began to creep across the basement as the creepers screamed at the sight of light.

Travis waved the flashlight's beam into the dark tunnel and motioned for his son to follow. The hatch had led to an underground tunnel, similar to those seen in prison escape movies or coal shafts. Ethan hands waved across the pitch black ground in front of him as he followed the sound of his father's scuffling.

They shambled along the tunnel for several yards. Ethan turned as a creeper fell into the hole. It howled as another landed atop of it. Ethan pushed his father forward as he began to crawl even faster.

"Whoa!" Travis cried as he could be heard falling several feet.

Ethan squealed as he lost track of his father's sound. The flashlight's beam disappeared from in front of him. His eyes darted about the pitch black as his voice wanted to cry out for his father. Panic raced through his mind as he felt the ground in front of him. Adrenaline surged through his veins as several flaming creepers began crawling through the tunnel behind him.

Ethan had never liked tight spaces. He never considered himself claustrophobic, but the walls began to feel like they were closing in on him. Ethan began to pant as he felt for the ground in front of him. Suddenly, his hand slipped as the ground disappeared into empty space.

"Ethan?!" Travis called out from the dark.

Ethan's heart raced with excitement at the sound of his father's voice. The creepers' hissing was growing closer as Ethan felt for solid ground.

"There's some sort of floor here," Travis explained. "I can stand up, but I lost the flashlight!"

Ethan wiggled his way out of the tunnel and fell into the empty space. His hands quickly clawed at the air as he fell. His body partially landed on what felt like a solid object and floor, before slipping into nothing. His right hand quickly snapped up the object as his left hand clutched the ground for dear life.

His legs dangled in the hollow space as his fingers pressed into what felt like compacted dirt. He realized what he was holding in his right hand and quickly turned it on. The flashlight's beam bounced off of a cavern wall and lit up the entire room.

The cavern shimmered with a golden glow as its reflective walls reflected light like a disco ball. Ethan was hanging for dear life from a naturally formed bridge, by one hand!

14

The bridge Ethan hung from was formed from dirt, grass, and sedimentary rock. Its soft surface was only made semi-hard by years of the earth's compacting weight.

The bridge stretched across the entire span of the cavern. The cavern itself was a uniquely earth-built shape as the walls rounded out the room and formed a natural dome. The walls were mostly smooth and consisted of tiny gold particles, reflecting any light.

"Ethan!" Travis yelled as he hurried to his son's aid.

Ethan tossed the flashlight onto the bridge and clutched his father's hand tightly. He dug into the ground with his left hand and pulled himself upwards with his father's support. Ethan rolled over onto the bridge and rested his head for a moment against the cool dirt.

He gazed over the edge of the bridge into the dark chasm. There was no end in sight. The chasm just seemed to keep falling deeper and deeper into darkness. Ethan stood up to see his father completely entranced by one last unique feature of the bridge.

In the middle of the bridge, the path widened out into a large circular platform. In the center of the platform was an enormous tree. It was alive and healthy as red fruit hung suspended from its branches.

This must be a ground-breaking discovery! A tree that can grow underground! What scientists would give to just learn about this specimen! Ethan peered over the bridge and saw that the tree's roots dangling in the air. There was no soil below the bridge, only empty space.

Ethan looked back at his father. Travis pulled a fruit from the tree and inspected its flawless design. Its beauty was like nothing he had ever seen. It was as red as a cherry, but as round as an orange. Its sturdy skin reminded him of that felt on an apple.

An inaudible voice began whispering into Travis' ears. It was followed by another whisper and another. Soon, multiple whispers began racing through his mind. Each competing over the other, to be the loudest voice.

Travis looked around, but no one was near him. Ethan was the only other person in this cavern and he was watching him from the far side of the room. Travis turned back towards the fruit. He wanted this fruit! Ethan seemed like nothing to him, compared to this fruit. It was all he could think about. All he *wanted* to think about.

The whispers continued to increase and support his decision. Travis wiped the fruit against his dirty shirt and stared at his own reflection displayed upon its crimson skin. The whispers' language was foreign to his ears but their message was not. Although indistinguishable, it was clear they wanted him to eat this fruit.

Ethan jumped back as a creeper fell out of the tunnel. He quickly snatched up his flashlight and waved it across the creeper. The beam sliced through its body like a blade as its frame turned to dust. Another creeper pushed itself from the tunnel and fell onto the bridge.

Ethan began retreating towards his father. Dirt began to fall from the cavern's walls around the tunnel. The creepers were burrowing through the tunnel. They were creating an even larger hole!

Ethan swung the flashlight and cut through the creeper's body. The creature shrieked as it dissipated in the air. Ethan backed into Travis and turned to see his father begin to raise the fruit to his mouth. A small black snake slithered down the tree and across Ethan's foot. Ethan jumped as he kicked the snake into the endless chasm.

Ethan smacked his dad's shoulder and Travis dropped the

fruit. His mind was suddenly cleared of the invading whispers. He didn't know why he had wanted that fruit. It's just a fruit! Especially at a time like this! What had gotten into his head? No matter. The whispers were gone and he was finally himself again.

Travis pulled Ethan back and motioned for the opposite side of the bridge. An entrance to a larger tunnel could be seen and Ethan nodded in affirmation. He handed his father the flashlight as he slid past him on the narrow bridge.

The bridge began to shudder as hundreds of creepers began pouring out of the tunnel. Some were still aflame from the basement and others looked like they were barely scorched. The one closest to Travis popped his neck from side to side as it began walking quickly towards its prey.

Travis swung the flashlight around and sliced through the creeper. Its face stretched ghastly in pain as its body turned to ashes. Travis swiped the beam across the horde as they began racing ever closer.

Suddenly a creeper sprinted through the pack and lunged for Travis' legs. Travis narrowly hopped over the creature's hulking body and turned to face another's growling face. Ethan screamed through his closed mouth as Travis was quickly becoming overwhelmed.

15

Travis snapped the flashlight upwards and cut through the intimidating beast. He turned and smashed the other's head into the ground, quickly stomping on its head again as he ran over its decomposing body. He stopped suddenly as he noticed Ethan's face turn completely white.

Travis turned to see the shaggy-haired man and Evelyn stand in the tunnel's entrance, smiling. Creepers raced around them as they stood, watching the two menacingly. The man jumped from the tunnel's opening and disappeared into the crowd of incoming creepers.

Travis began to turn back, before noticing one of the closest creepers. It was Katherine! She was still wearing her nightgown from when he had placed her in bed. Travis' throat began to constrict as he saw her hideously deformed face hunger for him and his son. That *thing* was not Katherine! Even though it was just another monster, Travis could not leave her. Ethan shook his head, but Travis ignored him and turned back towards the army.

Travis wrapped his fingers around the flashlight's handle and clutched it even tighter. He took several running steps forward, before swinging the flashlight across the front lines of the creeper army. The beam cut through Katherine's forehead and across her face. The cut sparked like coals in a fire, before her skin started to deteriorate into dust. The entire bridge rumbled again as Katherine stood, staring at Travis in astonishment.

"I love you," Travis whispered once more as the ground below them shook again.

The bridge fell from beneath their feet and Travis' arms snapped at the air. The flashlight fell from his hands as he tore at the air. He ran as quickly as he could up the falling bridge, before the rocks slid out from under his feet. Travis quickly grabbed a hold of a bundle of roots and clung to them for dear life.

His body slammed against the cavern wall. His failing arms shook as he tried to pull himself up the soft remains of the bridge. The smooth wall provided no surface to push himself up from. The only thing he could do was climb the decaying bridge remains by hand.

Suddenly, a hand pulled at his leg. Travis' hands slipped as he fell further into the chasm. The shaggy-haired man's dark eyes stared up at Travis as his jagged teeth were illuminated by the cavern's reflective walls.

The flashlight continued to fall deeper into the chasm, leaving the entire chamber to darken. Travis tried shaking the man off of his leg, but his grip was too strong. Travis kicked at the wall, trying to jar his grip loose, but it only served to loosen his own grip on the vines.

Travis took a deep breath and pushed himself off of the wall. The flashlight's illumination was completely gone now and the cavern was plunged into pitch black darkness. Travis's body slammed against the cavern wall and he could hear the man groan.

The man's jaws began snapping upwards at Travis' leg. Travis kicked off of the wall again and braced himself for impact. His shoulder smashed against the slimy walls as the man's grasp released. Travis sighed in a breath of relief.

With renewed strength he struggled against every aching muscle as he pulled himself up the soil's remains. His hands grasped for anything he could keep a solid grip on. His hand snatched upwards and grabbed ahold of a warm grip.

Ethan's hand wrapped around his father's and pulled him the rest of the way up. Travis panted as he fell into the tunnel's entrance. Ethan laid back against the tunnel floor and sighed. Moonlight crept through a trapdoor overhead, similar to the one they found in the basement. The climb was made easier by wood boards fastened to the wall, creating a makeshift ladder.

Ethan nodded as he noticed his father's relief. Suddenly, a hiss sounded from the entrance as the shaggy-haired man climbed into the tunnel. Ethan jumped to his feet as Travis gasped. Ethan landed a loud kick to the man's chest and sent him hurling into the endless depths of the dark chasm. The man shrieked as his screams fell quieter and quieter with increasing depth.

Ethan pulled his father up and wrapped his arm around his shoulder. Travis winced as he stood on his sprained ankle. Ethan motioned for his father to climb the ladder as he waited behind him. Travis pushed the panel up, but something heavy still rested on top of it. Travis pushed again and the large weight rolled off of the trapdoor.

Travis pulled himself up another two rungs and gasped. Ethan shuddered at the thought of more creepers as his heart stopped for a moment. He felt a sinking sensation in his chest as his eyes caught sight of the object of his father's horror. Travis turned back towards Ethan as his eyes filled with tears.

"Oh, no." Ethan's lower lip trembled as he regained the ability to speak.

He realized what his father had found. Tears began to stream down Ethan's cheeks as he stared up at his father. His heart literally slowed until it beat no longer. An overwhelming sense of dread and fear filled his body as his skin began to turn cold. Ethan's dead body lie bleeding out in the floor of the shed.

16

"No," Ethan cried as he felt every ounce of humanity begin to slip from his body. "I love you Dad."

Travis' eyes filled with tears as he stared at him. His son was alive, right in front of him, but somehow above, Ethan's lifeless corpse was covered in blood. His wrists were severed and blood leaked from the lacerations amassing the entire floor of the shed. The living Ethan in front of him was speaking and breathing. But how was this possible? How was his body right there? Like Katherine's? How were there two of them?

"I love you." Ethan cried one last tear before his eyes turned a dark black.

Travis shook his head in denial as the living Ethan crept closer. He shook his head again as the creeper opened his mouth to reveal multiple rows of razor-sharp teeth.

"No!" Travis shouted as he scrambled up the ladder.

He turned and quickly slammed the trapdoor behind him. He pushed a riding lawnmower atop the hatch and fell onto his knees. Tears fell down his cheeks in abundance as he picked up his son's body. He held his son's lifeless husk in his arms as he moaned in agony.

He could hear shuffling outside the shed doors, but it didn't matter now. His fight was over. His wife and son were dead. There was nothing left to fight for. His entire world had collapsed around him. He couldn't keep anyone safe. They had all died. Every last one of them. He couldn't save anyone. He promised Ethan he would save him, but he failed. That was the last promise he could ever make and it tore at him within his soul.

The door began to shake as Travis pulled his son's body closer. The creepers could find him, but they could never take him away from his son. Travis closed his eyes as the shed door swung open with a creak. He swallowed his fear as he waited for their pointed fingers to claw at his body.

"Dad?" a familiar voice called from the entrance.

Travis opened his eyes and slowly looked upwards. Christian stood in the doorway! He was clothed in his powder blue racecar pajamas and stared at his father with sincerity. The house behind him was blazing bright as smoke poured from the windows. Moonlight poured through the doorway, illuminating the child's blonde hair, as he looked pleadingly at his father.

"You're not real!" Travis shouted. "Quit toying with me! You want me? Here I am!"

Christian continued to look at his father in confusion. "Please?"

Travis' heart melted as the monster impersonating his son played his role so sincerely. His voice was identical to his son, retaining the very cracks in his voice that made him seem so innocent. Travis shook his head in denial as he pressed his lips against Ethan's forehead.

"No. No!" Travis shook his head vigorously as tears fell down his face.

"Please. Believe in me." Christian pleaded as he held out his hand.

The moonlight softly lit his small scarred palm. Travis looked up and gazed into the child's eyes. He looked so much like him. The recreation was flawless. He looked exactly like Christian! But if he was an impostor, how was he able to stand in the moonlight?

Christian's hair and palms were bathed in moonlight. Even the creepers had to stay in the shadows along the walls when they had chased Ethan and him earlier. Travis was confused, but realized the important decision he needed to make. He looked at his son's pale face once more and kissed Ethan's cold forehead one more time. He hesitantly stood up and took Christian's hand.

17

The riding lawnmower toppled against the shed's floor, as the creeper impersonating Ethan pushed open the trapdoor. He quickly climbed out and tackled Travis. Christian gasped as the two began wrestling in the yard.

The creeper's dark eyes stared into Travis' as his jaw began snapping at his face. Travis grunted as he held the monster's face away from his. He shifted the creature's weight and tossed him off of his body.

The creeper smiled as he picked himself up. He pulled his razor blade from his back pocket and swiped at Travis. Travis pushed Christian back as Ethan lunged forward. The blade slid across Travis' wrist as he held his arms up in self-defense.

Travis pushed Christian back a safe distance and charged at the creeper. The creature hissed excitedly as its prey was now giving it a challenge. The impostor quickly sidestepped Travis and sliced his opposing wrist. Its deadly precision was excruciatingly painful as Travis' wrists began to spill several drops of blood.

Travis turned around and growled in frustration. He coughed in the smoke-filled air as he stared down at the monster. The creature glared at him tauntingly with Ethan's face as it stood in the shadow of the shed.

Travis charged towards the creature once more, barreling into its chest. He knocked it to the ground and pinned it against the cobblestone walkway. He slammed his fist into its face. His knuckles connected with the creeper's taunting face, resulting in a solid crack.

He pounded another blow, followed by another into the creature's face. The impostor smiled amusedly as Travis pummeled its boneless face repeatedly. It began to laugh with a raspy, deep voice before changing tones to match Ethan's cries. The creature's face began to change into an expression of pain as a tear slid down its cheek. The dark eyes of the creature began to fade as Ethan stared up at his father.

"Please, dad. Please." Ethan's voice broke as he stared into Travis' trembling eyes. "Don't do this to me."

Travis held his fist back ready for another swing as he looked into the creature's eyes. Its lips trembled in fear as it waited in anticipation. Travis' arm quaked as he tried to force himself to see past the creature's sad exterior.

"Screw you!" Travis snarled as he grabbed the creature's shirt collar.

Travis stood up with a smirk as he removed the creature's

only defense. Moonlight fell upon the creature's tense body from behind Travis' shoulder as he stood watching the impostor writhe with agony. The creature shrieked as the moonlight began singeing its flesh, tearing away the façade of Ethan's face. Travis grabbed the creeper's burning face and slammed its head into the cobblestone path with a powerful crack.

The creature screamed as its skin burned with a red glow and quickly fell crumbled into ashes. Travis panted as he stood over the remains of his son's impostor. He fell backwards as the loss of blood from his wrists began to affect his body.

Christian rushed over to his father's side and cradled his head. "No! You have to get up. You have to!"

"Katherine." Travis murmured as he began to lose consciousness.

"No! Come with me!" Christian pulled his father's arm. "Come with me!"

Christian pulled his father up right and propped his back straight. Travis groaned as his body felt weak. He commanded his legs to move, but their tired muscles strained with response. Christian pulled Travis to his feet and wrapped an arm around his waist.

"Only a few more steps." Christian said, pointing towards the front gate.

"We can't leave." Travis said deliriously.

"Believe in me. I can save you." Christian said firmly, staring into his Travis' eyes.

Travis hazily nodded and shuffled towards the front gate. He rested wearily against the stone wall as Christian ran over and pulled the gate open. He turned back towards Travis and nodded accordingly.

Travis forced himself to take another step. He slid one foot in front of the next and stopped. He turned back to look at the house one more time. The entire house was amassed in flames. Its Victorian exterior cracked in the intense heat.

Travis spotted two figures standing side-by-side in the master bedroom window. The shadows resembled that of Katherine and Ethan, as their stern expressions stared coldly at Travis from within the burning house. The flames had not yet reached them, but soon the entire house would become a ruin.

The middle of the house fell inwards as several supports snapped from the unbearable heat. The walls of the house fell in upon themselves, as the raging inferno overtook the rest of the foundation. The smoke billowed slowly into the night air as Travis breathed in a shaky sigh of relief.

"Come with me." Christian said as he stepped outside the gate.

Travis pushed himself off of the stone wall and took another step. He stepped outside the surrounding gate of the house and felt the world around him begin to spin. He closed his eyes as he began to feel light-headed. The cold air whipped around his face as he felt like he was in the middle of a cyclone. Travis tried to open his eyes, but the whipping sting of the wind forced him to close them again.

18

After several seconds, the world began to slow in motion and the ground came to a standstill. Travis fluttered his eyes open as the cold air against his lips transformed into prickly blades of grass. He was lying on the ground! He didn't remember falling. Perhaps he had just passed out. He pushed himself up as his wrists screamed in pain. Ethan's blade fell from his shirt and onto the dark ground.

Blood trickled down his hands as he pulled himself upright. He groaned as every muscle in his body fought against him. Travis gasped as he blinked open his weary eyes. Tall pines surrounded the property as the surrounding wall had disappeared. He recognized the shed in the back corner of the yard, but yet it was distinctively different than that he had escaped from. Its tattered roof was supported by rusting red tin walls, as the aging building showed its age.

Travis rubbed his stubbly jaw as he stared in confusion at the nearby pool. He was standing in the backyard of a very familiar residence -his home in Los Angeles. His old home that held so many terrible memories and yet reminded him of the unbreakable bond this family held. He was wrong to have moved. The question was: Did they move? Why was he back here?

Travis kept his distance from the pool as he bounced up the

tiled steps of the back porch. He stood in awe for a moment as he stared at the house. The modern-style architecture was starkly different compared to the Victorian style of his nightmare. This was an average Los Angeles house. It was constructed with copious amounts of glass, but lacked the certain history that older homes boasted with pride.

His heart began to pound as he could hear the television through the glass walls. Travis stepped over a broken beer bottle and pulled the back door open, cautiously stepping inside. Travis quickly noticed a trail of water leading from the back door and decided to follow it into the living room.

Travis groaned as he brushed his hand over the familiar marble countertop. His wrists were still bleeding as he stained the white walls of his house crimson with streaks of blood. Travis grabbed nearby rags and tied them around his wrists. The sound of a crowd cheering erupted from the television in the living room as Travis pulled the rags tighter.

Travis' heart began to race as he hobbled into the dimly lit foyer. The television flickered with life as a football game played loudly in the silent house. Travis noticed several more beer bottles sat atop the coffee table as he searched for the remote. Travis grabbed a bottle and raised it to his lips as he flicked off the television.

His eyes began to widen as he felt a sticky substance stick to his hands. He rolled the bottle in his palm to see blood smeared across the label. Perhaps the blood from his wrists leaked onto the bottle when he picked it up, but something about the house felt off. It felt empty.

"Ethan?! Katherine?!" Travis called upstairs, setting the bottle back on the glass table.

Travis slowly walked up the dim stairwell as the stairs creaked with each step. He could hear the sound of water running from inside the bathroom at the end of the hall. Travis' heart began to race with hope as he briskly crept over to the bathroom door.

"Ethan?" Travis rapped his blood-stained knuckles against the closed door. "Katherine?"

Light poured out from underneath the door and cast a long shadow of Travis down the darkened hallway. Travis listened intently for a response as the water continued to run. Travis called again, louder this time, but no one answered. Travis shifted his weight eagerly awaiting a response as the carpet below him with a squish. He squinted in the dim light to see the carpet was a dark tan; darker than usual. Travis' heart raced as he realized water was pouring out from underneath the door, flooding the entire hallway.

Travis felt for the knob, but the door was locked. He quickly reared back and slammed an aching shoulder into the door. It cracked slightly, but still remained upright. Travis threw his weight against the door again splintering the entire door jam.

Travis stumbled inside the bathroom to find his wife's pale body floating inside the overflowing bathtub. Her skin was bloated as she had been lying in the water for some time now. Her dark purple lips contrasted repulsively with her bloodshot eyes, as they stared up at the ceiling without motion. She lay dressed in her finest cream gown as she floated about in the water. Her makeup was washing away as her cold hands clutched a dark blue hairdryer.

"No, no, no." He cried as he tried to force back tears.

He viciously yanked the hairdryer's cord out of the wall, before pulling Katherine from the tub. Travis fell back against the wood cabinets as he held his wife's corpse in his arms. His moans echoed throughout the hall as he sobbed over her still body. He held his wife's hand in his as his entire body trembled in pain. She had put her ring back on her finger. Her small fingers once again proudly symbolized their bond of marriage.

Travis shook his head angrily in denial. Why did she do this? Why? He loved her deeply, but that was never enough. After Christian's death, she had become so lonely and despondent. She could never look at any of them without remembering her lost child. She couldn't stand the remembrance of his death, but yet she hadn't wanted to move. Was this the price she was willing to pay? Was she capable of going to such an extreme in order to prevent leaving her memories of Christian behind?

His eyes caught sight of an object floating atop the water in the tub as he wiped his tear-stained cheeks.   Travis looked into Katherine's pain-filled eyes once more, before closing them slowly. He gently set her head against the white-tile floor, before stepping towards the overflowing bathtub.

It was a framed picture of the entire family. Travis held the photo in his shaking hands as he stared at the photograph. It was a happy moment captured in time as the family was laughing in the middle of a large park. Travis remembered the day quite clearly.

They had been playing kickball in the park, before kicking the rubber ball so far into the trees. Christian had run after the ball similar to a dog chasing after a thrown stick. After Christian didn't return for several moments, Travis went out to find him.

Within moments, the two returned to the field covered in mud. They had fallen into a massive puddle and were now dripping from head to toe in muck.

The picture showed Christian climbing over Travis' back as the family crowded near. Katherine's arm held the camera as Ethan was shown smiling into the lens. Their cheerful faces lit up the entire picture as a tear slid from Travis' cheek and onto the frame. Travis stomach began to sink as he realized the only sound in the house he could hear was the faucet running beside him.

"Ethan!" Travis cried as he charged into his son's bedroom.

The bed was a rumpled mess and clothes littered the floor. It was a typical teenager's room, consisting of cds and video games. The room was completely empty as was the entire house. There was no sign of Ethan. Travis could hear his own heart beat in his ears as his eyes caught sight of something outside the bedroom window. The soft moonlight danced upon the ragged roof of the shabby gardening shed.

"No." Travis cried as he forced himself out of Ethan's room.

Travis raced down the stairs and out the back door. His breath was heavy as he dashed across the yard. The blackened grass crunched underneath his feet as he quickly left the house behind him. He hadn't noticed it before, but the door to the shed was slightly ajar. The barely noticeable breeze rocked the door faintly. Travis slowed to a halt as a horrifying stench wafted through the air.

Travis pushed against his muscles, slinking closer towards the shed for a look inside. Gnats could be heard buzzing inside as the smell became more potent with every approaching step. Travis noticed a large handprint streaked across the door in blood. His hand snapped out and stopped the door from swaying, perfectly matching the bloody print.

Travis winced as he forced himself to keep from retching. He already knew what was inside the shed, but he had to be sure. Travis clutched his stomach as he peered inside the outbuilding. Ethan's lanky body lay slumped against a workbench. His wrists lay against his sides as their open wounds trickled blood onto the wood floor. Ethan's jaw lay open slightly with gnats flying around it, before they gently settled down, resting atop of his eye sockets.

Travis dropped to the ground as he stared at his son. Nothing made sense to him. Was it all a nightmare? Was it real? It didn't matter. He couldn't save them. He couldn't save any of them. He was wrong. The house wasn't his nightmare, this was. His mind began replaying his confession to Katherine. Had he ever confessed his true feelings to her? Why was he spared when they all left him?

Travis' head began ringing as he forced his eyes to stay open for a moment longer. His heavy eyes looked down at his wrists, which had slowly stopped bleeding. His body swayed with dizziness, before he fell against the hard ground. His eyes closed as the black grass crunched against his throbbing head.

He had missed the major arteries. He was a failure with nothing left. His family was gone. His mind was confused and his life no longer worth living. Why had he gotten a second chance? Why was he still alive and they were both taken? Why couldn't he save any of them?

19

Three Months Later

"This is it?" Lindsay groaned as she stared out of their sedan's freshly cleaned window.

"Would you quit complaining?" Andrea growled in frustration as she pulled the car to a slow stop, before parking.

"Only when you take me back home." Lindsay said defiantly.

"I can't." Andrea said, resting her head on the steering wheel. "I can't be with your father any longer."

"You guys never work anything out." Lindsay huffed, tossing her blonde hair behind her ear. "I'm sick of being caught in the middle of it all."

"Well you don't have to be any longer. Okay?" Andrea sighed. "We left him."

She was tired of fighting. She was tired of running. All of her life she had spent running away from something. An abusive stepfather, sexist bosses at work, previously failed relationships, and now her husband. It was time to quit running and finally settle down for once.

"You left him." Lindsay pointed out as she stared back out the window at the Victorian house.

"I'm just trying to do what's best for us." Andrea sniffled as she wiped her nose with her shirt sleeve.

Andrea sniffled and sat upright. She adjusted the rearview mirror to look at her daughter in the backseat. Lindsay stared out the car window as she pulled at the threads of her hoodie sleeve. She bit down on her bottom lip as she wiped away a tear.

"I'm tired of this attitude Lindsay. I'm trying." Andrea forced a hard lump down her throat before continuing. "We couldn't stay in that house. We . . . We just couldn't."

Lindsay glared at her mother's reflection in a fit of anger. Tears streamed down her red cheeks as she stared at her with a boiling temper. "I could've stayed! I could've. You need this! Not me!"

A light knock rapped on the driver's side window with a jovial energy. Both girls turned to see a smiling, middle-aged real estate agent waving to them.

Andrea shot a quick look at Lindsay and rushed to regain her composure. Lindsay rolled her eyes at her mother's ability to sweep things under the rug in order to seem pleasant to strangers. Lindsay sighed in disgust as she pushed the car door open.

Fall was beginning to settle and brightly colored leaves littered the street outside. Lindsay glared at her mother as Ms. Wiles introduced herself to the family. Andrea faked a smile and followed Evelyn inside the gated walls of Casa de la redención.

Evelyn chattered to Andrea as Lindsay began to hang back a few steps. Ms. Wiles pulled an old bronze key from her pocket and unlocked the front door. Lindsay groaned quietly as her mother began acting like a dumb blonde. It was never flattering, but Andrea did it to seem friendly to people she wasn't quite comfortable being around.

Lindsay sighed in disgust at her mother as she strolled around the finely kept lawn. She smiled as she took notice of the rickety shed alongside the house's surrounding wall. Its old tin walls shuddered in the breeze as a gust of wind blew around the corner of the house. Lindsay pulled open the shoddy door with a creak and took a look inside.

Everything seemed to have been tossed around the dusty floors, equipment lie everywhere with no real organization. There was an array of tools and gardening equipment stacked upon each other and a red riding lawnmower sat parked in the corner of the shed. Lindsay noticed a small metal object as it lay shimmering on the floor. She knelt down and picked it up.

"Ah, nice." She grinned as she inspected the razor blade.

She slid the razor blade inside her hoodie's pocket and closed the shed's door. Lindsay quickly sauntered back into the house, slightly worrying that her mother would lecture her about running off. Inside the house, she paused for a moment as Ms. Wiles began telling Andrea about the painting of the tree, inside the library.

All of the shelves were in their proper place and held countless numbers of aging books. Andrea moved closer to inspect the painting as Ms. Wiles took note of Lindsay watching. The older woman smiled wryly, before raising a burnt finger to her lips. Lindsay frowned as Ms. Wiles turned back toward Andrea and continued to explain the history of the house.

"Weird." Lindsay thought aloud as she strode across the foyer.

Her small hand rattled the basement doorknob, but the door was stuck. She began to leave before her sleeve's dangling threads became caught in the door jam. Lindsay pulled her sleeve from the door jam and ran her fingers along the side of the doorframe. The strike plate was disfigured in a similar way to wax on a candle. The door jam and lock now seemed as if they were melted into one solid piece.

A cold chill ran up Lindsay's spine, causing her to shudder. Her jittery spirit nudged her to continue the self-guided tour of the decrepit house. Before continuing, Lindsay decided to make a quick detour into the bathroom. Gently closing the door behind her, Lindsay took a deep breath and pulled a small plastic package from her hoodie pocket.

She tore the package open and poured the contents onto the side of the bathroom sink. A white powder fell from the packet and formed a tiny white hill on the sink's rim. Lindsay pulled the razor blade from her pocket and brushed the powder into a small line along the sink.

Lindsay bent down and took a slow steady breath. It had been a long car ride with too many talks about feelings and anger. She hadn't been able to calm down since they had left the house, originally. The powder tingled the inside of her nasal cavities as she inhaled a steady amount. She looked up at the ceiling, wiping away the powder from her nose, before looking in the mirror.

Dark circles lined her tired eyes as she stared at her reflection. She had never liked the way she looked. All of the other girls at school were always anorexic ally skinny and as pretty as a super-model. The best compliment she had ever received was that she looked like a ragged Sarah Michelle Gellar.

Lindsay had always kept to herself at school and even made a ritual of eating lunch underneath the busy stairs of Lawrence High. Everyone seemed to avoid her as news of her mother's exploits travelled around school quickly. There was no surprise that she was an accidental child and there was no surprise that her mother didn't want her.

Even though Andrea tried to seem like a mom, she was always interested in trying to find her next boyfriend. That's why it was astonishing when she reunited with Todd and remarried. Lindsay finally had a father and Andrea seemed to be settling down. Rumors at school began to die down as her mother was no longer a running joke.

Less than a year later, Andrea had begun to realize the life she had committed herself to. She decided she could no longer take the married life and ran away with Lindsay. Lindsay was still confused as to why her mother had even bothered bringing her. Maybe it was the only thing to ease Andrea's conscience as she began gallivanting across the country, but this wasn't what Lindsay wanted. She wanted a home, a family, and a father.

Lindsay's heart froze as her legs began to stiffen uncontrollably. Lindsay tried to lift her legs, but everything below her waist was now locked in place. Her chest began to pull from within her as she began to panic. Lindsay quickly brushed the powder into the sink and washed the remains down. If she needed to call for help, she couldn't allow her mother to know about her unorthodox anti-anxiety medication.

Lindsay struggled to move her legs again, but it was as if something strong had wrapped its powerful grip around Lindsay's legs. Lindsay cried as loud as she could for her mother, but nothing was heard. She tried yelling again, but she felt as if she had lost her voice. Lindsay looked up as her heart skipped a beat. Her pale lips had disappeared and her mouth was beginning to melt together completely.

Sweat raced down her forehead as she stared in silent horror at the mirror's reflection. The shaggy-haired man stood behind Lindsay and smiled at her menacingly. He turned his head to face the mirror and stare directly into her eyes. His pale skin was green in complexion as his eyes seemed to have the slightest hint of red. Their dark stare began to cause Lindsay's chest to feel as if it was caving in on itself. The man raised his finger to his thin lips and smiled. From behind her sealed lips, Lindsay took a deep breath and screamed as loud as she could.

Corvus Winchester

ABOUT THE AUTHOR

Corvus Winchester is a young aspiring writer whose dream is to write for a career. He found writing at a young age and since realized his love for storytelling. Please, please help his dreams come true!!!! Corvus Winchester is currently a college student working towards his computer engineering degree. He is a very curious individual and appreciates learning new things. His faith is very important to him and he feels it is expressed through his work. He enjoys playing guitar, reading books and short stories, hiking mountains, exploring new places, numerous types of art, and writing!!!

www.ingramcontent.com/pod-product-compliance
Lightning Source LLC
Chambersburg PA
CBHW070926130626
46555CB00001B/306